"Cooking relaxes me," Erin explained.

"Funny, it has just the opposite effect on me," he said.

"Your strengths obviously lie in other directions," she countered.

Steve had to admit he appreciated the way she tried to spare his ego.

"If you don't mind my asking, exactly what do you plan on making?"

"A frittata," she said cheerfully. Combining a total of eight eggs in a large bowl, she tossed in a dash of salt and pepper before going on to add two packages of the frozen mixed vegetables. She would have preferred to use fresh vegetables, but beggars couldn't afford to be choosers.

"A what?"

"Just think of it as an upgraded omelet. You have ham and bread," she said, pleased.

"That's because I know how to make a sandwich without setting off the smoke alarm," he told her.

"There is hope for you yet," she declared with a laugh.

Watching her move around his kitchen as if she belonged there, he was beginning to think the same thing himself—but for a very different reason.

* * *

**MATCHMAKING MAMAS: Playing Cupid.
Arranging dates. What are mothers for?**

Dear Reader,

Many articles have been written about the really difficult world of the single mother. But more and more I am beginning to see a new phenomenon emerging: the single dad. I see single fathers with one, two and sometimes three kids in tow, shopping in the grocery stores, looking haggard in the mall or on the street, going to or from stores while attempting to keep children in line—mainly by distracting them.

What started me thinking along the lines that this story eventually took was a letter from a single father to an advice columnist. He wanted to know where to find maternal-minded women. He had a small son and he wanted not just a wife but a mother for his boy (which I found extremely sensitive). She gave him some decent-sounding advice (none of which I could use in my story), but the seed was planted. I started thinking about all those fathers I've been seeing and wondering if they were married and if they weren't, and what did they do to try to fill not just one void, but two? Because, in essence, when a single father goes out on a date, he's really dating for two: himself and his child.

Since I am master (mistress?) of this universe I've created, my single dad's problems are solved by those three wonderful matchmaking mamas, Maizie, Theresa and Cecilia. Come and read their latest success story.

Thank you for reading and, as always, I wish you someone to love who loves you back. You have that, you have everything!

Best,

Marie

Dating for Two

—

Marie Ferrarella

HARLEQUIN®SPECIAL EDITION®

ISBN-13: 978-0-373-65824-4

DATING FOR TWO

Printed in U.S.A.

MARIE FERRARELLA

This *USA TODAY* bestselling and RITA® Award-winning author has written more than two hundred books for Harlequin, some under the name Marie Nicole. Her romances are beloved by fans worldwide. Visit her website, www.marieferrarella.com.

To
Allison Carroll
for displaying concern
over and above
the call of duty.
Thank you.

Prologue

That was the third time Maizie Sommers had caught her client staring off into space in the past half hour.

Eleanor O'Brien had come to the real-estate agency that Maizie owned several weeks ago. The middle-aged, sweet-faced woman wanted to downsize her lifestyle, replacing her thirty-year-old two-story house with a more space-efficient condominium. Maizie had given her the benefit of her expertise, instructing her on how to present her home to its best advantage. The crash course had definitely paid off. There were already several buyers not just interested in Eleanor's house but ready to make an offer.

Eleanor had decided to hold off accepting one until after she'd found a condo that caught her attention.

But today, apparently, her attention was elsewhere. Maizie had taken her to three different condominiums today and she had the impression that her client was there in body, but her mind seemed to be a hundred miles away.

Initially, she had politely ignored Eleanor's preoccupation. But there was no sense in showing her these homes if she wasn't really seeing them.

"If you don't mind my saying so, you seem rather lost in thought," Maizie told the petite woman with the frosted blond hair. "You know," she went on tactfully, "we don't have to see these condos right now."

Maizie wasn't just pretending to be thoughtful of her client's sensibilities—she really was concerned. She'd taken to Eleanor in these past few weeks and she prided herself on being a people person first, a Realtor—something she was exceedingly successful at—second. Or third if she counted the vocation she really had a passion for—matchmaking.

While she made her money being a Realtor with a very successful track record of matching the right person to the right home, her heart was even more firmly entrenched in her matchmaking endeavors, something she did on a joint basis with her two very best friends, Cecilia and Theresa, both accomplished businesswomen in their own chosen fields. Friends since third grade, the women enjoyed bringing happiness into people's lives by matching them up with their soul mates. So far, *that* track record was stellar.

"If there's anything I've learned in my years of selling homes," Maizie went on as her client looked at her quizzically, "if you miss out on one, no matter how perfect it might seem, another one will be by soon enough—sometimes when you least expect it."

Eleanor O'Brien laughed softly to herself. "That sounds like a slogan for a dating service, not a real-estate office."

Maizie found it interesting that the first thing on her client's mind was a reference to dating. Was that what was bothering the woman? Something to do with dating? Maizie's radar was instantly engaged.

She linked her arm through Eleanor's, subtly guiding the woman back to the condo's front door. "Why don't we take a break and go somewhere for a cup of coffee—or tea if you prefer—and you can tell me what's really on your mind."

For a moment, Eleanor looked torn between thanking her—coupling it with a protest that she was fine—and taking her up on her offer.

As it turned out, it was a very short internal debate. The woman's need for a friendly ear to talk to won out.

"Well, if you're sure that I'm not taking you away from anything else—"

Maizie flashed what one of her friends had referred to as her "disarming" smile. "You're not," Maizie assured the other woman.

Eleanor nodded just as they reached the door. "Then yes, I think I'd like that."

Maizie smiled. "I know just the place."

Ten minutes later, seated at a table for two in a family-friendly restaurant near Maizie's office, Eleanor leaned in and asked her, "Do you have any children, Maizie?"

Maizie felt a sudden rush of maternal pride, the

way she always did when she thought of her only child, Nikki. "As a matter of fact, I do," she replied. "I have a daughter."

Eleanor's eyes met hers as she asked, "Is she married?"

Maizie smiled. She liked to think that her daughter was her very first real success story. Because Nikki had been so very caught up in her career—she was a pediatrician—her daughter had had no private life she could call her own. That was, until inspiration hit and Maizie had deliberately sent one of her clients, a widower with a toddler, her way. The rest, as people like to say, was history—and the beginning of a very gratifying matchmaking sideline.

Maizie never brought up what she thought of as her "true calling" unless the situation warranted it. However, she was beginning to get some very specific vibes from the woman sitting across from her that this just might be the case.

"Yes," she told Eleanor, "as a matter of fact, she is."

Eleanor sighed wistfully. "You don't know how lucky you are. I have a daughter—Erin—and I don't think she is *ever* going to get married."

"By choice?" Maizie asked as she studied her client. After all, there *were* women who were quite happy not having to take a husband's choices into consideration whenever they wanted to go somewhere or do something.

"By attrition," Eleanor replied sadly, then attempted to backtrack. "I suppose I'm being selfish. I should just be grateful that I still have her." Seeing Maizie's questioning look, Eleanor realized how enigmatic that had to sound. She was quick to explain. "When Erin was seven years old, she came down with a form of cancer." She closed her eyes, revisiting that painful time. "We came very close to losing her a number of times. She lived close to two years at that wonderful, groundbreaking children's hospital in Memphis. During that time I almost wore out my knees praying.

"And then one day, all traces of her cancer miraculously disappeared and I got my little girl back. I can't describe the joy her father and I felt." Tears shimmered in her eyes as she relived what she was saying. "That's why I feel so guilty wanting more."

"But?" Maizie prodded, sensing the woman needed just a little encouragement to continue.

Eleanor inclined her head. "But I would love to see her married with children of her own."

"She doesn't have a steady boyfriend?" Maizie guessed, just to make sure that wasn't the problem.

"She doesn't have *any* boyfriend," Eleanor answered with a heartfelt sigh. "She's too busy." Maizie's client pressed her lips together. "Even her choice of careers is selfless and I know I should be happy she turned out this well—"

Maizie had been in the same place herself once, so she felt justified in interrupting her client. "You have nothing to feel guilty about. It's only natural to want to see your daughter with someone special in her life, someone she can lean on." Inspired, Maizie's mind began going in several different directions at once. "What does your daughter do for a living?"

"She owns a toy company called Imagine That,"

Eleanor said with no small pride. "She sells the kind of toys that you and I had as children—the kind that need imagination instead of batteries to make them come alive. Twice a year she takes a whole truckload of toys and brings them to the local children's hospital. Erin says it's her way of 'giving back.'"

Maizie nodded her head, impressed—as well as eager to help. "She sounds like a wonderful person."

"Oh, she is," Eleanor said with feeling. "And I desperately want her to know the joy of holding her own child in her arms." Again guilt rose its head within her. "I suppose I'm being selfish…."

"Not at all." Maizie waved away the sentiment. "I've been exactly where you are."

Eleanor looked at her with surprise. "You have?"

Maizie nodded her head. "Absolutely."

"Did you do anything about it?" Eleanor asked, lowering her voice as if they were discussing a possible conspiracy. It was obvious that she was searching for some sort of advice or at least encouragement.

Maizie smiled over her cup of coffee. "Funny you should ask," she began. She saw the hopeful expression that came into the other woman's brown eyes. She signaled the waitress, and she told the young woman when she approached, "We'll need to see two menus, please." This was going to take some time, she decided. Then, turning back to Eleanor, Maizie got down to business. "Have I got a story for you."

Chapter One

"There you go," Steven Kendall said as he handed Cecilia Parnell the monthly check he had just written out to her company. "And it was worth every penny," he freely admitted to her. "The job done by your house-cleaning service would even pass my mother's stringent inspection, and trust me, my mother has always been a very tough little lady to please," Steve attested.

Time and distance gave him the ability to look back at that part of his life fondly, although at the time, living through it as a teenager had been exceedingly difficult for him.

Cecilia smiled at the young business-litigation lawyer. He'd been a client of hers for a little more than a year now and she had never known him to be anything but cheerful. It was literally a pleasure doing business with the man, especially since he took no exception with what could be seen as an idiosyncrasy: she liked to be paid in person.

Cecilia laughed softly. "All my clients should be as difficult to clean up after as you and your son," she told him. "And just because I don't mention it, don't think I'm not grateful that you don't mind indulging me and maintaining this personal aspect of the process." She tucked the check away into one of the many zippered compartments within her rather large hobo purse. "I know most young people your age prefer going the digital route—your internet bank account communing with my company's internet bank account—but I must say that I really do like the personal touch." She flashed a self-depreciating smile at Steve. "I know that must seem hopelessly old-fashioned to you."

. The woman's words struck a familiar chord. "To tell you the truth, Cecilia, I could do with a little more 'old-fashioned' these days."

Something in his voice caught her attention. "Oh?" Cecilia gave him her best motherly smile as she set down her purse again. "You are my last stop of the day, which means I'm free after this, so if you need a friendly ear to talk to, I can certainly stay awhile."

Her maternal smile took in Jason, Steve's seven-year-old, as well. The boy spared her a marginal glance before getting back to what had become his main focus during his waking hours when he was home: killing aliens that popped up on the family-room TV monitor.

"It's not often that I find myself in the company of two such handsome young men," she went on to say.

For a moment, Jason's attention was diverted—an unusual occurrence these days, Steve noted. "Is Mrs. Parnell talking about us, Dad?" he asked.

A sliver of hope went through Steve. Maybe Jason was finally coming around. Mentally, he crossed his fingers even as the boy went back to vigilantly guarding humanity against the alien threat.

"Well, you, at least," he told his son. He doubted that Jason even heard him. He was back to playing his video game.

"Oh, don't sell yourself short, now, Steven," Cecilia told him. At her age, her words could be seen as complimentary rather than flirtatious, which allowed her the freedom of not having to watch every word she said. "You are a very good-looking young man—which leads me to wonder why you're here, talking to me, instead of going out. It is Friday night and unless my memory fails me, this is considered prime dating time for unattached men of your age bracket." She glanced at Jason. "If you need a sitter, as I've already said, I am available," she offered, knowing that the woman who watched Jason until Steve came home from the office had just left for the day.

"No, thank you. I don't need a sitter and your memory is very sharp, Cecilia." He knew that the woman was aware of his particular situation. Rather than feeling as if she were invading his privacy, he was touched that she cared enough to be concerned about him. "I've decided to back away from the dating scene for a while."

Cecilia frowned slightly. She'd taken a personal interest in the young widower and his son. She couldn't help herself—he seemed as if he needed just a touch of mothering since his own mother lived some distance away in another state.

"Correct me if I'm wrong, Steven, but didn't you just reenter the dating world a couple of months ago?"

Cecilia formed it as a question, but she knew perfectly well what his answer to that was. After two years of doing nothing but working and spending time with his son in an effort to shut down the sharp pain he'd felt over losing his wife, Julia, to uterine cancer, the personable lawyer had given in to his friends' entreaties and started dating again.

What had gone wrong? she wondered.

And how could she help?

"Technically, you're not wrong," Steve told her. He walked into the kitchen and opened his refrigerator. He took out a bottle of orange juice and poured himself a small glassful. "I did reenter the dating world, although it was more like four months ago than just a couple. In any case, now I've decided to *un*-reenter it."

Of the three lifelong friends, Cecilia had always been the most soft-spoken one. But being around Maizie and Theresa had caused her to be a little more aggressive in her approach toward people, a little bolder when it came to speaking her mind. Prior to their foray into the matchmaking world, she would have never had the nerve to say what she said now.

"If you don't mind my asking, why would you do that? You're in the prime of your life and heaven knows, a good, solid man like you would be the answer to many a lady's prayer." When he looked at her in surprise, she quickly added, "I have a couple of good friends who bend my ear about their children's inability to connect with the right person."

Although accurate, her explanation was a little dated. Up until several years ago, she, Maizie and Theresa would get together at least once a week for a friendly card game and a session of seeking mutual comfort regarding what they all viewed as the plight of their unmarried daughters. It was at one of these sessions that Maizie first decided that they needed to do more than just talk, lament and worry. They needed to take a proactive approach to their daughters' situations.

Since all three of them had businesses that allowed them to interact with a broad spectrum of people, they decided to make use of that and *find* husbands for their daughters, setting them up without either parties involved realizing that they *were* being set up.

They succeeded so well that they just continued dabbling in the matchmaking business even after they ran out of their own offspring.

Now every time she or one of her friends came across a single person without a significant other at least in the wings, the wheels in their heads began turning.

The way they were doing right now.

About to walk out of the kitchen, Steve remained where he was and lowered his voice. He didn't want Jason to overhear.

Once he began talking, Cecilia understood why.

"I'm not cut out for this anymore," Steve confided in her.

The man was handsome, intelligent and sensitive. If ever a man *belonged* out in the dating world, looking for his soul mate, it was Steve.

"But why?" she asked sympathetically, her manner quietly urging him to unburden himself.

"All the women I've gone out with in these past few months have been very attractive. Not only that, but for the most part, they were also smart, funny, motivated career women," Steve told her.

So far, there seemed to be no problem. However, she was well aware that life was seldom just smooth, untroubled sailing.

"But?" Cecilia supplied the missing word she could hear in his voice.

Steve flashed a weary smile. "But as soon as they knew I had a son, they all reacted in one of three ways. Some were upset that I even *had* a son and ended the evening, saying there was no future for us. Others equated having children with being fitted with chains, something they made clear they wanted no part of. And the ones who were open to the idea of kids equated having a child with having a cute pet— *not* the way I view Jason," he told her with feeling.

Steve sighed and confessed, "Absolutely none of these women were even remotely what I'd consider to be 'mother material.' I guess when I entered the dating arena, my situation was rather unique." Before she could ask him what he meant by that, he told her. "I'm not just dating to date—I'm actually dating for two. Any woman I see socially has to be willing to not just see me but to take Jason into consideration, as well. He's part of my life. A very *big* part of my life," he said, looking over his shoulder at the boy, who was now deeply engrossed in his game. "Since none of the women seemed willing to see it that way, I've decided to take an indefinite break from dating." And then a smile filtered into his eyes and he said, "Unless, of course, you'd like to go out with me. Tell me, Cecilia, what are you doing for the rest of your life?"

Cecilia laughed and shook her head. "Getting older, dear," she replied, patting his cheek, "but that was a very sweet, ego-boosting thought on your part and I'm flattered."

She paused for a moment, debating something. She looked over toward Jason. The boy was lying on his stomach, ignoring everything around him and focused completely on the learning video on the monitor. His thumbs were all but flying across the controller in his hands.

When Steve had opened the refrigerator, she'd had occasion to look in. It hadn't been a promising picture. Which was what prompted her now to ask, "When was the last time you had a home-cooked meal?"

"That all depends," he replied.

That was a strange answer, Cecilia thought. "On what?"

Steve grinned. He would have been the first to admit that while he was very successful in his chosen field and liked to dabble in a number of different "hobbies," cooking was definitely not among them, unless burning food could be considered a hobby.

"On how broad a definition of the term *home-cooked* you mean. If you mean a frozen dinner warmed up in my home microwave, then my answer is yesterday. If, by chance, you mean something out of the oven that didn't come out of a package from the frozen section of the grocery store, then my answer would have to be the last time my mom came to visit, three months ago."

Cecilia nodded. "That's what I thought. Let me see what I can come up with," she told him. She pushed up the sleeves of her blouse and opened the refrigerator again.

Granted, he was hungry, but there was such a thing as imposing and he didn't want to ruin the relationship he had with this woman. He liked talking to her.

"I can't have you do that," Steve protested, stepping in front of her and attempting to close the refrigerator again.

She cheerfully moved him aside and got back to foraging. "Consider it a bonus for being such a good client."

Maizie, Cecilia thought as she got down to business, was going to love this guy.

"What's his name again?" Maizie asked that evening as she, Cecilia and Theresa got together.

It was an impromptu meeting. Cecilia had called both of her best friends the second she had gotten into her car. She'd just left Steve raving about the casserole she had made out of the odds and ends that she had found in his refrigerator and his pantry. Even Jason had been moved to say something positive after being made to pause his game and come to the table to eat.

At that point she was feeling particularly good about the plan forming in her head.

All she needed was help from "the girls."

They met at Maizie's house within the hour.

Maizie was currently sitting in front of her laptop, ready to try to get as much information as she could about this potential candidate that Cecilia felt seemed overdue to find love again.

"His name is Steven Kendall," Cecilia told her, then spelled out his name carefully.

"You know him—do you think that Steven might have a page up on Facebook?" Maizie asked, already pulling up the site.

"I don't know about Facebook," Cecilia replied. "He seems friendly enough, but he is a rather private person when he's not working."

"What does he do?" Theresa asked.

"He's a lawyer specializing in business litigation and—" Cecilia got no further.

"A lawyer?" Maizie echoed. It wasn't so much a question as it was a triumphant declaration. "That means he's probably got a photo and a profile online with his law firm."

Pulling up a popular search engine, Maizie lost no time rapidly typing in the man's name. She leaned back in her chair as Steve's photograph and minibio came up on screen. She was clearly impressed.

She emitted a low whistle and said, "Not bad, Cecilia. Not bad at all."

Curious, Theresa leaned in over Maizie's shoulder to get a look at the man. "Not bad? If I were ten years younger, *I'd* give him a tumble myself." She glanced up to see the skeptical, amused looks on both of her friends' faces. "Oh, all right, twenty years," Theresa corrected.

"Better." Maizie laughed. "Besides, I've already got someone for him," she told Theresa as well as Cecilia. When Cecilia had called her, she hadn't had a chance to tell either of her friends about Erin O'Brien yet, but she quickly filled in the details now.

Finishing, she looked back at the lawyer Cecilia had brought to her attention. Her smile was wide and infinitely hopeful. "If you ask me, this seems like a match made in heaven. She's a toymaker who loves children and he's a widower with a child who by definition loves toys. It doesn't get any better than this."

Neither of her friends disagreed. "But how do you suggest we go about bringing these two made-for-each-other people together without them knowing it was a setup?" Theresa, ever practical, asked.

Maizie chewed on her lower lip for a moment as she gave that little problem her undivided attention. "The difficult we do immediately. The impossible takes a little longer," she said, reciting an old mantra.

"That's Maizie-speak for nobody goes home until we come up with a plan for them to meet," Theresa said with a sigh, bracing herself for a long night.

Maizie patted her friend's hand as she rose to her feet. "You know me so well. I'll put up a pot of coffee," she told her friends before crossing to the kitchen.

* * *

Erin O'Brien hung up her phone, still a little bewildered at exactly how Felicity Robinson had gotten her name, much less her phone number. But then, she supposed in this day and age of rampant nonprivacy, anything was possible for someone with a reasonable amount of tech savvy if they were determined enough. And if there was one thing she had come away with from this conversation, it was that the assistant principal of James Bedford Elementary School certainly sounded extremely determined.

"Guess what," Erin said to the friendly-looking stuffed T. rex on her desk, one of several that she owned. The T. rex had been the first toy she'd ever made, and the original, now rather shabby for wear, was locked away in a safe. "We're going back to school. Seems that somebody wants me to talk to a roomful of seven-year-olds about how I got started making toys."

She cocked her head, giving the T. rex a voice in her head and having him make up excuses for why they couldn't go. The T. rex embodied her insecurities. He always had. It had been her way of dealing with them as a child.

"Oh, don't give me that snooty face," she said, addressing the dinosaur. "You're a ham and you know it. This'll be fun, you'll see," she promised, using almost the same words that the assistant principal had when she'd called her.

"Yeah, for you," the high-pitched voice whined. "Because you'll say anything you want through me."

Erin leaned over her desk and pulled the stuffed

animal to her. Affectionately dubbed Tex the T. rex, the stuffed dinosaur had been her start, her very first venture into the toy world. Imagination—a *positive* imagination—had been her crutch, her way of dealing with all the things that had been going on in her young world when life had consisted of machines that whirled and made constant noise at different frequencies while they measured every kind of vital sign they possibly could via the countless tubes that seemed to be tied or attached to her little, sick, failing body.

Even back then, though shy, she'd possessed an inner feistiness. She'd done her best to be brave so that her mother wouldn't cry, but even so, Erin was firmly convinced that if she hadn't invented Tex—her alter ego as well as her champion—when she had, she would have broken down rather than triumphed over the disease that had threatened to end her life more than once all those years ago.

Tex had started out as a drawing and was, for the most part, a figment of her imagination until she had given him life by utilizing an old green sock her mother had brought her.

Somehow he managed to stay with her—in spirit and in drawings—all the way through school. A while later, she decided to give Tex a better form. Her mother went to a craft store and bought green felt, and Erin had had stuffing. Armed with a needle and thread as well as a black Magic Marker, she brought the dinosaur to "life" one fall afternoon.

From that day forward, in one form or another, Tex had remained with her.

A chance comment from a child in an on-campus

day-care center was ultimately responsible for her creating a friend for Tex—Anita. Anita was equally nonmechanical. Equally gifted with a soul via Erin's imagination.

And suddenly, Imagine That was born.

"And now we get to tell a cluster of second graders all about you," Erin told her stuffed animal with pride.

"Don't forget the part where you would be nowhere without me," "Tex" reminded her in that same high-pitched version of her voice.

"I won't forget," she promised, saying the words as if she were actually carrying on a conversation with another human being.

She indulged in the little charade mainly when none of her staff was around, so that they wouldn't think she was losing her mind if they happened to overhear her in effect talking to herself. It helped her knock off steam when things got tense, but she could see how it might unnerve someone witnessing her exchanges with herself.

"We made it, Tex. We made it to the big time—or to the little time, if you will," she augmented with a grin.

For once Tex said nothing.

But she knew what he was "thinking." The very same thing she was. That they had truly "made it" in more ways than one.

Chapter Two

Steve hung up the landline phone in the kitchen and looked over at his son. Jason, as usual, was in the family room, his attention glued to the action on the TV screen.

"Did you have anything to do with this, Jason?" he asked.

"To do with what, Dad?" his son responded after he repeated the question a total of three times. As had become his habit, Jason was only half paying attention to anything going on outside of the video game he was playing. The game had become an all-important obsession for him, something he did with most of his waking hours unless his father made him do mundane things like eat and sleep and go to school. Aside from that, he could be found before the TV in the family room, defeating aliens and making the universe safe for another day.

He was not about to relax his vigilance, convinced that slacking off for even a second would bring about dire consequences. It could bring about the end of life as he knew it, as *everyone* in his world knew it. He couldn't allow that to happen. Not on his watch. He'd already lost his mother; he couldn't afford to lose his father or his grandmother, as well.

"I was just on the phone with your assistant principal," Steve said, nodding toward the receiver he'd just hung up. "She asked if I'd speak to your class on Career Day."

He sank down on the sofa. Jason's thumbs were going a mile a minute on the controller. The TV monitor was filled with dying aliens that disintegrated into tiny purple clouds before vanishing altogether.

Steve couldn't help wondering if his son had even heard him. "I didn't know you had a Career Day."

Jason shrugged, his small shoulders rising and falling in an exaggerated motion since he was lying on his stomach. "I guess so," he mumbled.

Without Julia, his late wife, as a buffer, Steve had found himself groping around, trying to find his way in his son's world. Every time he thought he was making just a tiny bit of headway, something would happen to show him that he hadn't made any at all.

But he couldn't give up now, because the next thing he said might be just the right words that would help him to get through to the boy. Above all, he wanted to keep their relationship open and honest—so he asked a lot of questions. But he didn't get a great deal of feedback.

"She sounded desperate, so I said I'd do it. Is that okay with you?" he asked. The last thing he wanted to do was embarrass his son, no matter how persuasive the woman on the other end of the line had come across.

"It's okay, I guess," Jason said with no real enthusiasm. Then, turning to look at him over his shoulder, his son added a provision to his agreement. "As long as you don't kiss me around the other guys."

Steve suppressed a grin. Now, *that* he could fully relate to and understand. He could remember how embarrassing parental demonstrations of affection could be at that age. "It'll be hard, but I promise I'll control myself."

"Good." Jason nodded. Going back to killing aliens, the boy asked absently, "Whatcha gonna talk about?"

"My career." Then, because of the perplexed look on his son's face when Jason turned toward him again, Steve added, "I'm a lawyer, remember?"

"I 'member," Jason answered almost solemnly, then asked, "You gonna do some lawyer stuff for the class?"

There were times when he felt that Jason didn't have a clue as to what he did for a living. Julia liked to say that he argued for a living. He supposed that was as apt a description of his profession as any. But he doubted that a group of seven-year-olds would understand the joke.

"I'm going to explain to your class what a lawyer does," he told Jason.

"Oh." It was clear that Jason didn't seem to think that would go over all that well with his class—but he had a remedy for that. "Maybe you better bring treats, like Jeremy King's mom did when she came to talk about her job."

He honestly considered Jason's suggestion. "Maybe I will bring treats since food seems to be the only thing that impresses people your age."

The aliens still weren't dying and the controller remained idle in Jason's hands, telling Steve that he had his son's full attention—at least for a half a minute more. "I like chocolate, Dad."

"Yes, I know," Steve said with as straight a face as he could manage.

And then the consequences of his affable agreement hit him. He was going to have to stand up in front of a classroom full of restless little boys and girls and try to hold their attention for at least ten minutes, if not more. Steve looked over toward the phone he'd just hung up on the wall. Maybe he'd been just a little too hasty saying yes.

Oh, he had no trouble standing up before an audience. Most of all, he was really apprehensive that he might inadvertently embarrass his son—which in turn might push the boy even further away from him than he was now. Seven-year-olds were sensitive and desperately wanted to blend in, not stand out, and having him in the classroom would definitely single Jason out.

"So you're okay with my coming to your classroom?" he asked again.

"Uh-huh."

Steve gathered from his son's tone that Jason was once again clearly engaged in the business of knocking off tall, thin gray aliens and was a million miles away from him.

A few days later, Steve was still having second thoughts about talking in front of Jason's class. Actually, his second thoughts were into their third edition at this point.

But if nothing else, he was well aware that it was too late to pull out. He had committed to this speaking engagement and he was nothing if not a man of his word.

It was a lesson he was trying to teach Jason and he knew if he bowed out at the last minute, aside from leaving the assistant principal high and dry, he would be teaching Jason that it was all right to give your word and then break it on a whim.

He might not be the world's best father, but at least he knew that much was wrong.

Jason's teacher, Mrs. Reyes, had placed two folding chairs in the front of the room, putting them a few feet away from her own desk. The intention was that the speakers wouldn't feel as if they were "on" the entire time. Her aim was to afford the speakers a clear view of the classroom and its occupants, even while keeping everything at a safe distance.

Steve took his seat, wondering who else had been

roped into this "sales pitch to seven-year-olds," as he had come to think of the experience.

He didn't have long to wait for an answer. No sooner had the question occurred to him than the classroom door opened and he heard a rather melodic, softly compelling voice say, "I'm sorry I'm late. I'm afraid my staff meeting ran over."

"I'm just glad you could make it," Mrs. Reyes said, smiling broadly at the owner of the voice. There was more than a measure of relief echoing in the teacher's own voice.

Steve turned to look at the late arrival and found himself suddenly and completely captivated. The young woman, carrying what appeared to be a wide valise or case of some sort, was all swirling strawberry-blond hair, bright blue eyes and heart-warming smile.

Unlike him—he was wearing a light gray suit— she was dressed casually in a light blue summer dress that brought out her eyes even more than nature already had. To top off the picture, the woman had the best set of legs he'd seen since—well, he couldn't quite remember since when.

"Hi," the woman said to him as she took the seat beside his. Her eyes swept over him as she asked, "Are you giving a Career Day speech, too?"

"Yes." Suddenly at a loss for words, all he could do was smile at her—and feel utterly inept. Something that had *never* happened to him before.

"What's your career?" she asked in a deliberately low voice. She was intent on not distracting anyone in the classroom; however, the low timbre managed to distract Steve big-time. "Well, you're in a suit, so it must be something important," she assumed, then made a guess. "Doctor?"

He barely shook his head. The rest of him felt as if he had been frozen in place, trapped in her eyes. Who *was* this woman? "No," he breathed.

"Lawyer?" was her second guess.

"How did you know?" There was no *L* on his forehead, no aura particular to lawyers. He couldn't see her managing to figure it out on her second guess.

She smiled and he found himself even a little more captivated than he already was—if that was possible. "The old nursery rhyme. You know—rich man, poor man, beggar man, thief. Doctor, lawyer, Indian chief. You said no to doctor and you didn't look like a chief, so I took a stab at lawyer." That out of the way, she asked the next logical question. "What kind of a lawyer are you?"

"A good one," he replied.

His own answer sounded almost flippant to him—and that just wasn't like him at all. He was good, fair and dedicated. None of those attributes had any leeway for flippant.

"Ah, one with a sense of humor. That's good," she pronounced with a smile that for a moment rivaled sunbeams.

The next moment, she was leaning into him. "Which one's yours?" she asked in a hushed whisper that at the same time seemed incredibly sexy to him, given the circumstances and where they were.

Could a voice in a second-grade classroom even *be* sexy? Steve couldn't help wondering.

"That one over there, the towhead with the cow-lick," he told her.

It took her a second to find the child he was pointing out. "Very handsome boy," she told him with a nod of her head. Steve knew what she'd just said was a standard reply and maybe it was just his imagination, but she seemed to mean what she said.

"Which one's yours?" he asked, thinking it only fair to put the same question to her.

"Oh, I don't have one in this class," she replied.

He found that odd. Weren't you supposed to have a kid in the room before you could address said class?

"Then—?"

As if anticipating the rest of his question, the woman beside him said, "The assistant principal thought it might be a good idea for me to come by today and address the class."

Steve came to the only conclusion he could. The woman had to have a unique career.

"What's your career?" he asked outright, unable to even venture a guess, especially not one that would involve a valise.

She opened her mouth, apparently to answer his question, when Mrs. Reyes spoke up and by the very act commanded that they all give her their undivided attention.

"Well, it's my favorite Wednesday of the month again. Career Day," she emphasized with feeling. "And first we will hear from Jason Kendall's father, Steven Kendall, who is going to talk to you about what it means to be a business lawyer." Turning toward him with a bright, welcoming smile, Mrs. Reyes said, "Mr. Kendall, the floor is yours."

With that, Mrs. Reyes gestured around the classroom, in case he missed her meaning.

Steve rose and instantly became aware that his legs felt a little stiff. The last time he'd felt that, he recalled, he'd been in court, pleading his very first case. He'd won, but only by a hair, and while others might have become cocky because a win was a win, his win humbled him because he knew how close he had come to losing that first case.

It was then that he realized that things were decided by the whimsy of fate and although he was always prepared, always did his best, he never lost sight of that humbling lesson.

Coming before the class now—Mrs. Reyes had vacated her desk, so he stood behind that as he spoke—Steve remembered beginning, remembered his mouth moving as his brain raced from point to point, trying to hit all the points he'd jotted down for himself earlier.

He was acutely aware that while his audience of seven- and eight-year-olds all sat at their desks listening politely, not a single face in that audience looked the least bit interested, much less inspired by either his vocation or anything that he had just said to them.

Not that, he silently admitted, he had said anything terribly interesting or inspiring.

And certainly not very memorable.

When he was finished, applause came after a beat. Polite applause as if they had been coached to applaud anyone who appeared to have stopped talking. He was glad to reclaim his chair and sit down.

"And next we have Ms. Erin O'Brien." Instead of announcing the next career, Mrs. Reyes smiled at her class. "You're in for a treat," she promised. "I think you'll find Ms. O'Brien's career *very* interesting." Mrs. Reyes looked toward the next speaker, exchanging glances with her as if they had a shared secret. "Ms. O'Brien, the class is all yours."

Rather than the young woman saying anything in response to Mrs. Reyes, another voice was heard. A muffled voice as befitting one that came from inside a suitcase.

"Hey, it's dark in here, Erin. Lemme out."

Erin's hooded eyes covertly took in the room. Apparently, she had the entire classroom in the palm of her hand as children exchanged giggles and nervous glances with one another.

Erin looked at the valise on the floor next to her chair. She had a pseudoexasperated look on her face. "Tex, I told you to be on your best behavior."

"This *is* my best behavior," the voice coming from the valise insisted.

"If I let you out, you have to promise not to scare the children," she warned.

"Children?" the voice asked, sounding very intrigued. "Tasty children?"

"That's something you're never going to find out. Now, do you promise to behave?" she asked.

The voice sighed. "Do I hafta promise?" Tex whined.

"Yes, you do," Erin said, crossing her arms before

her as she continued talking to the "occupant" of the valise. "I'm afraid if you want to come out, Tex, that's the deal I'm offering. Otherwise, you'll have to stay in the suitcase until we leave."

There was another, louder sigh from the inside of the valise. Then the voice said, "Oh, okay, I guess. I promise."

"That's all I wanted to hear," Erin told the voice.

Snapping the locks open, Erin quickly took out the valise's mysterious occupant. The latter turned out to be a large green dinosaur whose head was bigger than his body, in direct contrast to an actual model of a *Tyrannosaurus rex*.

This T. rex was also wearing a white cowboy hat, which was in keeping with his Southern twang.

Once in her arms, Tex did an exaggerated long visual sweep of the boys and girls seated at their desks. "I know I said I'd behave, but can I just nibble on that little one over there?" The puppet nodded vaguely to his left, pretending to drool.

"No, you cannot," Erin insisted. "We came to *talk* to these nice kids."

"You talk, I'll nibble," Tex said, leaning over as he eyed certain children.

Erin drew herself up and gave the dinosaur a very stern look. "Tex, do you want to go back into the valise? Think carefully now."

The puppet hung his head, ashamed. "No, ma'am, I do not."

"Okay, then no nibbling," she pretended to order him sternly. Her eyes swept over the eager young faces on the other side of the room. As always, a feeling of gratification washed over her.

Tex, however, was ever crafty, ever hopeful. "Then how about—?"

She shot the T. rex down before he could mention a single name—she'd taken care to ask for a seating chart and the names of all the children when she'd agreed to giving a talk. Using names made everything ever so much more personal.

"No."

The dinosaur was nothing if not persistent. "Not even—?"

"No," she said emphatically, cutting the T. rex off before he was finished.

The children's laughter grew with each interaction between the woman and her puppet. "Now remember why we're here," she told the T. rex.

Drooling again, the dinosaur eyed his potential snack. "You remember. I'll chew."

Erin gave the puppet her very best glare. "Tex, you're impossible."

"No, I'm very possible," he assured her. "But I'm also just very hungry. Hear that?" He looked down at his midsection. A noise was heard. "That's my tummy growling," he protested. Instead of the rumbling of an empty stomach, an actual lion's roar echoed through the classroom, bringing more giggles.

Steve had to admit that he was as captivated and as hooked as the children were, except that to them, the exchange between the strawberry-blonde woman and the dinosaur in her arms was very real, while he found himself enthralled by an extremely good ventriloquist who was very easy on the eyes.

He watched her lips—something he realized he became caught up in with great ease—and couldn't really see them move, yet he knew that somehow, they *had* to because the exchange was so lively.

In the end, Erin gave, all in all, a very entertaining "talk."

She had brought more characters with her, toys that had hitchhiked in the valise only to jump out—with a little help from her—in a semiorderly fashion when she called to them. Some of these characters spoke, some did not, but the running thread through all the toys she did display was not a single one of them required a battery, a power strip or even a windup key of any sort.

All they uniformly required, Steve discovered, was imagination. Imagination by the bucketload.

The other thing that the toys she'd introduced had in common was that each and every one of them—and she almost presented them as family—was initially her brainchild. Toys that came into being out of some childhood adventure or childhood need to keep the darkness at bay.

The young woman with the talking green dinosaur had created all the toys she'd brought with her, Steve thought. He found himself being more than a little impressed by her efforts, her creativity and her very real dedication to jump-starting children's imaginations again. Moreover, though she didn't come out and say it, he got the impression that Erin O'Brien had put together and built up her toy company all on her own, not an easy feat in this day and age.

He couldn't help but admire her determination. A man could learn from a woman like that.

And so could a classroom full of energetic seven- and eight-year-olds.

Chapter Three

The woman really did have a way about her. While the second graders had listened to him politely, there had definitely been a certain lack of enthusiasm among them.

He didn't really blame them. Very few seven-year-olds aspired to be lawyers—as a matter of fact, he doubted if there were *any* seven-year-olds who even remotely contemplated that. He would have had to have been something along the lines of an astronaut in order to have sparked their imaginations.

But the moment Erin O'Brien took center stage—even before her T. rex started "talking," he saw a definite shift in the pint-size audience. They appeared to be hanging on her every word, anticipating something funny or just plain fun. It was almost as if they seemed to sense what she was about to do—entertain them by bringing make-believe into their world.

Steve found himself mesmerized by her, as well. But what *really* caught his attention was when he glanced in Jason's direction and saw that his ordinarily solemn son's face was animated, that he was taking in everything she said.

And when Tex requested "just a teeny, tiny taste" of one of the children in the audience, he was stunned to see Jason laughing. Actually laughing.

Jason hadn't laughed since Julia had died.

Steve could feel his heart constricting within his chest. When he'd lost his mother, the light had simply gone out of Jason's eyes. Not only that, but his entire personality had undergone a drastic change. He had become introverted, retreating into the world of video games. He'd completely stopped playing with his friends, stopped everything that even vaguely reminded him of a time when his mother was still around.

While it worried him, Steve was afraid to push the subject, afraid he might make things worse. His friends advised him to give Jason time.

But how much was enough? No one had an answer, least of all him.

And meanwhile, here Jason was, responding to a make-believe dinosaur and the woman who had given that T. rex life. It left Steve in utter awe. So much so that it took him a minute before he realized that Jason's teacher was saying something to all of them.

"—and I would like to thank both Ms. O'Brien and Mr. Kendall for coming in this morning and taking the time to talk to us about what they do for a living," Mrs. Reyes concluded.

The next minute, Erin was leaning into him, keeping her voice low as she prompted, "I think she wants us to stand up now."

Like a pop-up toy on a three-second delay, Steve quickly rose to his feet. He managed to effectively cover up his chagrin. He'd been so wrapped up in his discovery and his thoughts about Jason that he hadn't been paying attention to what the teacher was saying.

He flashed a quick smile at the older woman, who looked pleased. "Class, how do we say thank you to these two nice people?"

In response to her question, the children began to clap.

"Thank you for your attention," Steve said, acknowledging their applause.

"Maybe next time, you'll have some tasty snacks for me," Erin said in her best Tex the T. rex voice.

The class clapped harder as they laughed and cheered.

"You certainly know your audience," Steve told her in an aside.

"I was a kid once," she said by way of an explanation. "Weren't you?"

"I can't remember," he answered, tongue in cheek.

He noticed that the valise she had brought with her seemed to be bulging excessively despite the fact that she had brought samples of the toys her company put out and those were now safely in the hands of her audience. The valise appeared almost too bulky for her to handle.

"Here, let me help you with that," Steve offered as he pushed open the classroom door so that she could walk out first.

"That's okay," Erin demurred, crossing the threshold. She switched hands, taking the valise into her left one in order not to bang it into him. "I've been lugging around Tex and his friends since before they had a toy factory to call home."

Steve wasn't about to take no for an answer. He closed the classroom door behind him and caught up to her in less than two strides. "Still, it would make me feel like a Neanderthal if I watched you struggle to your car with that."

"You could try closing your eyes," she suggested.

"This works better," he countered, slipping his fingers deftly into the small space on the handle that she wasn't currently holding.

Erin was about to pull the valise a little closer to her, telling him that she was fine and it was no big deal, but then she shrugged, deciding to surrender the suitcase rather than play tug-of-war with it.

She had to stop constantly trying to prove to the world that she wasn't the sickly little girl anymore, she silently lectured herself. The voice in her head sounded oddly like her mother.

"Wouldn't want you to feel like a Neanderthal," Erin said as she let him take the valise. "I'm parked right out front."

And then she remembered. "No, you're not."

The voice actually *did* seem as if it came out of the valise. Steve paused, looking from it to her. "Your suitcase is arguing with you?"

"Sorry, I do that sometimes when I'm nervous. Tex puts me on a more even keel," she explained.

"You're nervous?" he asked, amazed, thinking she was referring to having to speak in front of Jason's class. "You certainly didn't act like it."

"That's why I have Tex." Actually, she'd been fine talking to the class. She related to children. Her problem was talking to adults. *That* made her nervous. But he did seem like a nice man. At least he hadn't said anything about her behaving strangely.

"I just remembered that I'm not parked right out front—I had to park by the curb. The school parking lot was full when I arrived. They really should have more parking spaces," she said as they walked out of the building.

Steve looked around. She was right. All the parking spaces in front of the school were filled with vehicles.

"I guess when they built the parking lot, they didn't count on so many of the sixth graders driving," Steve quipped.

He had a sense of humor. She liked that. "They must not be automatically promoting them to the next grade unless they can pass their tests."

He pretended they were having a serious conversation and deadpanned, "I guess not."

"My car's right over there," Erin said, pointing to a small, economical-looking white Civic that had seen its share of miles. She unlocked the driver's-side door, then flipped a lever to unlock the other three.

She noted that Steve was still holding her valise. "You can put the suitcase right there," she prompted, and then smiled when she caught the surprised look on his face. She could almost see what he was thinking. "You think my car should be fancier, don't you?"

By the looks of it, the car was about seven years old or so and while it wasn't dented, it did appear weathered.

"I just thought you looked more like the sports-car type."

"Nope, not me. Besides, Jeffy runs very well," she said, patting the car's hood. "He was there for me when I needed him and I tend to be very faithful if something comes through for me."

Was she just talking about her car, or did she mean that in general? he wondered. The women he'd encountered lately all seemed to be interested in "newer, fancier, better." Sticking with something reliable didn't seem to be in their game plans. He was drawn to this woman with the funny voices.

"Do you name everything?" he asked.

"Mostly," she answered seriously. "But only if their personality comes through—or the name fits."

He had to admit he was intrigued. "And just how does *Jeffy* fit a Civic?"

"The letters in the license plate." To prove her point, Erin rounded the car and pointed to the rear plate, a combination of numbers and letters. The letters read JFF. "JFF is very close to Jeff, which is close to—"

"Jeffy. I get it," he concluded, then nodded, amused. "Interesting thought process." Not to mention that she was a very interesting woman.

He realized that if they went their separate ways

right now, chances were that he would never see her again. He didn't find that acceptable.

Outside of his law practice, he was a fairly low-key, easygoing man who definitely wasn't pushy, which was why he hesitated now.

Still, nothing ventured, nothing gained, and he'd heard Jason laugh earlier. That *definitely* deserved further investigation.

Steve caught the driver's-side door as she was about to get into her car. She looked up at him quizzically.

"Listen, I cleared my morning because I wasn't sure how long this Career Day thing was going to last, so I don't have to be back in the office until after lunch. Would you like to go somewhere and grab a cup of coffee or tea or something?" Because she wasn't saying no, he added, "There's a great little French bakery/café not too far from here."

Catching her bottom lip between her teeth, Erin glanced at her watch. There were things she had on her agenda for this afternoon and ordinarily, she didn't just go off with a man she'd met less than an hour ago. As gregarious as she seemed around the children, around adults she was an extremely shy person who struggled to sound as outgoing as she knew she was perceived.

For heaven's sakes, it's a café, not a sleazy bar in some rough neighborhood, a little voice in her head coaxed. *Your mother's always after you to get out more. This qualifies as "more" since you're already out of the office. Go for it!*

Steve saw her looking at her watch and hesitating.

"I'm sorry," he said. "I guess I thought that since I didn't have to be back until after lunch that you were free, too. You probably have to be somewhere right after your talk."

He's giving you a way out. Take it, she told herself. *Take it!*

Still...

"Well, not right after," she allowed.

"Great," he responded with a wide smile that she found instantly appealing. "Why don't I just get my car and you can follow me to the café—unless you'd rather I drove you there."

She liked the fact that he didn't immediately try to dominate the situation. "I always loved multiple choice—I'll follow you," she decided, feeling better about having her car with her—just in case things didn't go well. It was hard making a quick getaway if her car was two miles down the road.

"Stay right there," he told her as he began heading toward his own car.

"Can't very well follow you if you're not there to follow, now, can I?" she called after him, amused.

"Right." Still walking, Steve turned around so that his voice would carry to her. "Be right back," he promised.

As he hurried off, all he could think was that if any of his clients had been privy to this less-than-suave behavior, they'd have second thoughts about having him represent them in anything, much less in a courtroom. But while his professional behavior was decisive, intelligent and sharp, the private Steve

Kendall was not nearly as dominant or forceful as the public one.

Julia had spoiled him. They had been the proverbial childhood sweethearts—he'd known he wanted to marry her when he was all of thirteen years old, even though it'd taken him another eighteen months to work up the courage to steal a kiss.

That had clinched the deal—for both of them.

There had been no dating other girls, no oats, wild or otherwise, that he'd wanted to sow. All he'd ever wanted was to be Julia's husband and the day he proposed, Julia confessed that she'd never even *thought* about marrying anyone else but him. They were made for one another. Consequently, he had never had to endure and suffer through the rigorous training camp known as dating.

That was why, he reasoned, he came up short now, why he just wasn't any good at this whole dating-ritual thing. Even though he did his best to channel his professional persona into his private life whenever possible, he would be the first to admit, albeit only to himself, that he just didn't really know what he was doing.

Small talk was particularly difficult for him.

But even though they had said only a few words to each other, Erin seemed very easy to talk to. And, far more important than his own comfort, he could see that she'd made an impression on Jason. Or at least, she and her T. rex had.

That made this an avenue he had to explore—for both Jason's sake and his own.

Pulling up to where Erin was still waiting for him,

he rolled down his window and said—needlessly, he realized as soon as the words were out of his mouth—"Okay, you can follow me now."

"I thought you'd never ask." She laughed, starting up her car. She fell into place right behind him.

The café he'd told her about was in the middle of a very small strip mall, nestled between a five-screen movie theater that guaranteed low admission prices for their slightly-less-than-newly-released movies and an art studio that prided itself on bringing out the budding artists buried within the five-to-ten-year-old students who attended.

It seemed like a nice area, she judged. Best of all, there was more than ample parking available, so when he pulled into a spot, she was able to park right next to him.

He got out of his vehicle and quickly hurried over to hers so that he could open the door for her as she started to get out.

Chivalry was not dead, she thought to herself. This was nice.

"It doesn't look like much," he told her as they crossed the lot to the front of the café, "but the pastries practically float off your plate and the coffee is the best around. I can't speak for the tea, though," he added, apologizing.

"That's all right, I'm really a coffee drinker at heart," she told him.

The scent of freshly brewed rich coffee mingling with the aroma of freshly baked cakes and pastries greeted them the moment Steve opened the door for her.

Erin could feel her mouth watering the second she walked in. Between the aroma and the display of baked goods just behind the glass that ran the length of the counter, she was a goner.

"Well, there goes my diet," she cracked. "I think I gained five pounds just by inhaling."

"What is your pleasure?" the older woman behind the counter asked politely.

Erin looked at the pastries, each one more tempting than the last. "One of everything," she told the woman wistfully.

Though pleasant, the woman behind the counter looked as if a sense of humor was not part of her makeup.

"That can be arranged," she said in a very serious voice.

Afraid that the woman would begin placing things on the tray that Steve had picked up and was resting on the counter right now, Erin quickly shook her head.

"Oh, no, no, I was just kidding, giving voice to a fantasy," she explained. Taking a breath, she scanned her choices one last time and made up her mind. "I'll have a cup of coffee and a cream-filled turnover."

"Make that two," Steve told the woman.

The dark-haired woman inclined her head. "As you wish," she replied.

With a grand sweep of her hand, she indicated that they should move along to the center of the counter, toward the register. She met them there, delivering two cups of steaming, aromatic black coffee and two large cream-filled turnovers, each residing on its own plate. The woman carefully placed the plates one at a time on the tray, right next to the coffee.

She proceeded to ring up the sale. "Will that be together?" she asked.

"No," Erin answered.

"Yes," Steve said at the same time, his voice resounding slightly louder than hers. Taking out a twenty, he handed it to the woman.

"No, really, this isn't necessary," Erin protested, reaching into her purse.

The woman seemed to take no note of her, handing Steve his change. He slipped what she'd given him into the tip jar beside the register and picked up the tray. For the first time, the older woman smiled.

"You don't have to pay for me," Erin told him as he walked over to a small table for two to the left of the register.

Setting the tray down, he looked at her. "If you had asked me out for coffee, I would have expected you to pay for me," he told her cheerfully, despite the fact that he really wouldn't have allowed her to pay. The idea of going Dutch had never appealed to him and it wasn't something he felt comfortable about doing. Certainly not when it came to something as insignificant as a cream-filled turnover and a cup of coffee. "Tell you what," he suggested, sitting down after she had taken her seat. "You tell me what fantasy you were giving voice to and we'll call it even."

She looked at him, slightly confused. "What?"

"Back there, when that woman looked like she was more than happy to give you 'one of everything,' you stopped her by saying you were only 'giving voice to a fantasy.'" As he spoke, he distributed the two cups of coffee and then the two turnovers. With the tray empty, he removed it and put it out of the way on the floor behind his chair. "Did you used to dream about pastries?"

He meant it as a joke, in the same vein that he'd asked her about naming inanimate objects. He hadn't really expected her to answer his question seriously.

"All the time," Erin told him with a heartfelt sigh.

"You weren't allowed sweets as a kid?" he asked. The guess arose out of his own childhood, when one of his friends—Billy—had parents who wouldn't allow him to have any candy, cake or cookies. Billy's snacks were all painfully healthy foods, such as nuts, fruits and carrots. The second Billy was out of the house, he made up for it, scarfing down as many sweets as he could get his hands on. He'd had a serious weight problem by the time he was twenty.

Erin, on the other hand, looked as if she was in danger of blowing away if she lost as little as five pounds.

"Oh, I was allowed sweets," she told him. "I just couldn't keep any of them down."

He took a sip of his coffee before venturing, "Allergies?"

Erin broke off a piece of the turnover and savored it before answering, "Chemo."

"Chemo," Steve repeated, stunned. "As in chemotherapy?"

"That's the word," she acknowledged, nodding her head. Even now, more than twenty years later, the very sound of the word brought a chill down her spine. She always had to remind herself that she had conquered the horrible disease, not the other way around.

He felt as if he had opened his mouth as wide as possible and inserted not just one foot but both. "I'm sorry, Erin. I didn't mean to bring up any painful memories."

She smiled at him, appreciating his thoughtfulness. "You didn't. I was the one who brought up the memory—you just asked about it."

How did he extract himself without sounding clumsy—or callous?

"Are you all…better?" Well, that certainly was neither suave nor warm, he upbraided himself. "I'm sorry. This is none of my business—"

"That's all right," she assured him. "I don't mind answering. Too many people act like you're some kind of alien creature when you have cancer. They don't know what to say, so they don't say anything at all—and they just disappear out of your life. As to your question, yes, I'm all better, thanks for asking.

"And it wasn't all bad," she confided. "Being that sick made me appreciate everything I had, everything I was able to enjoy after I got out of the hospital. Besides, if it wasn't for that whole experience, I would have never met Tex."

"Tex," Steve repeated, drawing a blank for a second. And then he remembered. "That would be your stuffed dinosaur, right?"

"Hey, who're you calling stuffed?"

The high-pitched voice caught him off guard and

he automatically looked around to see where the voice was coming from before he realized that Erin had projected it.

Erin tried hard not to laugh. "I'm sorry," she said, her eyes still dancing with amusement. "I just couldn't resist. Tex has been such an integral part of everything I do, at times I have to admit I almost feel he's real."

"That makes two of us," he told her.

Even so, Steve was only vaguely aware of her apology. What he was far more aware of was that Erin had placed her hand on his wrist while she was talking to him.

The second she'd touched him, he had felt an instant connection with this animated, unique woman.

Chapter Four

His interest engaged and heightened, Steve found himself wondering things about her. A great many things. For starters, he was intrigued by the wording she'd used in referring to the puppet that had created such a hit with the class.

"Just how did you 'meet' Tex?" Steve asked. Then, before she could begin to answer, he quickly added, "And if you don't mind, I'd rather you told me the story instead of hearing it from Tex."

Instead of taking offense, the way he was afraid she might, Erin laughed. "Sure. I didn't mean to make you feel uncomfortable by using his voice," she apologized.

He didn't want her to think he was humorless. "I'm not exactly uncomfortable," he told her, searching for the right way to explain just what he *did* feel. "I guess

I just feel a little strange having a conversation with a suitcase—especially when the suitcase is still out in your car," he pointed out.

"Well, at least you're not hoarse from shouting," Tex's voice told him. And then Erin flashed a very endearing chagrined expression. "Sorry, I just couldn't resist one parting comment."

"Maybe you're missing your true calling," Steve speculated.

She wasn't sure where he was going with this. "And that would be?"

"Stand-up comedy with Tex and those other toys you brought with you." And that reminded him of something else. Sitting across from her like this had all sorts of thoughts as well as questions popping into his head. "By the way, that was very generous of you." When she raised her eyebrows quizzically, he elaborated, "Bringing enough toys for the whole class."

Erin raised one shoulder in a shy, dismissive shrug he found startlingly appealing. "It's actually a little selfish of me."

"Just how do you figure that?" Steve asked.

To her it was as plain as day. "Easy. I get back a lot more than I give. There's nothing greater than seeing the joy bloom on a kid's face and knowing that you were partially responsible for putting it there." Before he could respond, she quickly changed the subject, returning to a previous comment he'd made. "And as for your suggestion about doing stand-up comedy, I do get to satisfy that whim twice a year when I pay a visit to CHOC—Children's Hospital of

Orange County." Erin was quick to spell out the full name in case he wasn't familiar with the facility or its common abbreviation.

"Twice a year?" he echoed. She really *was* serious about bringing joy to children, Steve thought. "Let me guess—around the holidays."

"Obviously nothing gets past you," Erin teased.

"You were going to tell me how you and—" Steve lowered his voice without realizing it "—Tex met."

Erin stared at him. "Why did you just do that?" she asked with a laugh.

"Do what?"

"Lowered your voice before saying 'Tex.'"

The second she said it, he realized she was right. He'd lowered his voice automatically, the way he would have if he were talking about Jason with the boy close by. Steve had no choice but to laugh at himself and the situation.

"Because now you have me acting as if that puppet of yours is actually real," he confessed.

She took it as a compliment in part and smiled her thanks. "Then I guess I do owe you that explanation. I created Tex to keep me company. When the doctor diagnosed me with cancer, I didn't know what it was, but I knew it was scary enough to frighten my poor mother. She tried not to let me see, but she did a lot of crying. Then someone told my dad about that famous children's hospital in Memphis. My mother lost no time in getting me in. My dad stayed back home working while my mother flew out with me.

"The people there were all very kind," she recalled with fondness. "But treatment is a long, frightening process when you're a little kid. I missed my friends back home. They sent messages and we stayed in contact for a few weeks, but that didn't last long and little by little, it stopped." She shrugged, avoiding his eyes. "I felt like they forgot all about me. I wanted a friend who would always be there for me whenever I was scared or lonely—my mother told me I would never be alone as long as I had my imagination."

"Smart lady," he commented.

Erin smiled. "She is—when she's not being a mother hen. Anyway, I was really into dinosaurs, so I created Tex. At first he was just one of my thick green socks that I drew a face on with a laundry marker. Then my mother got some green felt, and I bought sequins and pillow stuffing in a craft store. I sewed him by hand at my bedside and drew in his features." She smiled as she remembered the early prototype. She still had him locked away in a box in her closet. "Tex wasn't very pretty but he was very, very loyal, which was all I wanted.

"I held on to him when they took me in for my treatment sessions." Despite the amount of time that had passed, the memory was still very vivid in her mind. "And he never left my side no matter how sick I got. After a while, I really did start thinking he was real. Since I couldn't go anywhere, I created some fantastic adventures for us in my head. All that helped get me through some of the darker times," she told him, trying to make the whole experience sound less of an emotional roller coaster than it actually had been. After all, she wasn't trying to elicit his pity just to fully answer his question.

"After I miraculously got better, I started to think about other kids who had to go through what I did. Other kids who might have felt abandoned, lonely and scared. I wanted to help them get through it, just the way Tex helped me. That desire never left me, so while I was still in college, I came up with the idea of creating a whole line of stuffed dinosaurs that didn't do anything but look loving. And with each stuffed toy, I'd include a little book of adventures that the toy and the child who got that toy would have. I donated the first hundred I made to a local hospital's children's wing."

He could easily see her doing that. He had clients who would have had heart failure over the mere suggestion of giving away their product like that. She had an extremely large heart, he couldn't help thinking.

"Not very profitable," he commented.

"Oh, there was profit," Erin assured him with feeling. "Profit in ways you can't begin to imagine. Seeing those bright, happy faces was absolutely priceless. And I felt I was giving a little something back to a medical system that cured me. Anyway, it turned out that a local newscaster's son was among the kids in that hospital who got one of my dinosaurs. The newscaster did a story on me. Pretty soon that segment was being picked up by other station affiliates and before I knew it, the story had gone national and I was getting donations to create more toys and more books."

Erin smiled at him as she finished off the turnover she'd been picking at. "And just like that, I was officially in the toy business. It didn't hurt that parents who weren't dealing with the trauma of severely ill children were ready to introduce plain, old-fashioned imagination back into their children's lives. I was getting in more demands than I could fill by myself. That was when I decided I needed help and hired a couple of people I'd gone to college with. Pretty soon a couple of people weren't enough to keep up with the demand, so I hired a couple more. Now I'm so busy I have to schedule brushing my teeth." She flushed. "I guess that's more information than you wanted."

Actually, he found himself wanting even more, but he kept that to himself for now. Rather than address her last sentence, he commented on her time crunch. "You seemed to have found time for Career Day."

She laughed. "I have trouble saying no to short people," Erin told him.

"Kids or Mrs. Reyes?" he quipped.

Her eyes crinkled as she smiled at the question. She'd meant children, but she could see his point. "Mrs. Reyes was rather petite, wasn't she? Actually, it was the school's assistant principal who called me. A woman by the name of Felicity," she remembered. "When she told me that the presentation would be in front of a classroom full of second graders, I just couldn't get my lips to say no." Her shoulders rose and fell in a disparaging shrug. "So I didn't."

When she'd referred to her lips, Steve's eyes were drawn to that part of her and he caught himself wondering, just for the slightest moment, how they might feel against his own.

The next moment, he silently scolded himself. What was the matter with him? *You're not in the market anymore, remember? You tried dating and you're just not any good at it or at picking suitable candidates. Stick with what you know—being a lawyer.*

Dating someone made him feel like a fish out of water. Granted, this little break with this woman was exceedingly nice, but he couldn't exactly call it a "date." If anything, it was a pleasant interlude, a pause in his normally hectic routine. He couldn't think of it as anything more than sharing some coffee with a really nice fellow human being.

Nothing to be made of that, he reminded himself.

"I have to admit that I was a little envious, watching you."

"Envious?" she asked, surprised. "Why?"

"The kids looked as if they were hanging on your every word."

She was quick to correct his observation and put it in its proper perspective. "They were busy eyeing all the toys, hoping to get their hands on some."

He knew better. "Those kids all took to you even *before* you started handing out the toys. You had that whole class in the palm of your hand the second you started talking."

She saw it differently. "You mean the second *Tex* started talking. I wasn't an adult speaking to them— I was Tex's keeper." Which was just fine with her. "Kids are more than willing to suspend reality and believe in talking dinosaurs or anything else that sparks their fancy. That's the trick," she told him with a discernible measure of pride. "Sparking their fancy, making them your partner in the world of make-believe. Kids love adults joining them in this world where they can have great adventures and where absolutely *anything* is possible.

"To be completely honest, I love it, too," she told him, "because it allows me to experience—vicariously—what I wasn't able to experience when I was that age."

Using a minimum of words to refer to herself, she had managed to create an image in his mind of the little girl she had once been. She'd aroused both his sympathy and, more importantly, his admiration. She'd not only survived everything that had happened to her but managed to find some good in it and use what she'd found to help other children faced with those very same daunting conditions.

"Well, whatever the pragmatic explanation is, all I know is that my son really took to you—and Tex."

She liked the fact that he tagged on the dinosaur, even if it was as an afterthought. To her it meant that he had a large capacity not just for empathy but for flexibility, both of which were important qualities as far as she was concerned.

"Your son." She paused for a moment to picture the class in her mind. "That would be the quiet one with the beautiful green eyes?" Eyes, she now noticed, that father and son seemed to share.

"That would be him. Jason," Steve said, giving her his son's name. "I haven't seen him that enthralled with anyone—or anything—in two years."

Erin knew she should be going on her way, but this man with the magnetic green eyes had managed to pique her curiosity with his last comment. Children were definitely her weakness.

"What's been going on these last two years?" she asked him, even as she wondered if she'd overstepped some hidden line.

"Not very much of anything," he confessed. Finished with both his turnover and the coffee, he slipped the plate from one under the saucer of the other. "The sitter I hired brings Jason home from school and he goes right to the TV monitor in the family room."

The boy was around seven or eight. "Cartoons?" she guessed.

Steve shook his head. "Video games," he told her. "Except for when I get him to do his homework, he's glued to that set in the family room, playing this one particular video game where he has to shoot down an army of aliens to keep them from destroying the earth."

Erin was vaguely aware of the video game he was referring to.

"Noble endeavor," she commented, then couldn't help adding, "Sounds a little bloodthirsty for a seven-year-old, but noble."

"The game's actually labeled age appropriate," he told her. He had made sure of that, but once he actually saw Jason playing it, he had his doubts. Unfortunately, the boy appeared hooked on it. "Besides, compared to the way he'd been right before he started playing, I was thrilled that he showed an interest in *anything*.

"Unfortunately, trying to get him away from the game, other than when he's in school or in bed, is impossible," he confided. "In a way, it's as if this is the only reality Jason can deal with. That's why when I heard him laughing this morning, it was like suddenly seeing the sun coming out after enduring forty days and nights of nonstop rain."

Instead of basking in the implied compliment, Erin was far more curious about what had caused this withdrawal in his son in the first place. She had a feeling she was treading on private ground, but she sensed that the man sitting across from her needed to get this out, needed to talk about what was bothering his son—and very possibly him, as well.

"What happened approximately two years ago?" she asked Steve quietly, her voice low, coaxing, her eyes unwaveringly on his as she did her best to make him feel that it was all right to share this with her.

Steve took a deep breath before speaking, as if that could somehow shield him from the pain the words always created.

"Julia—Jason's mother—died."

Sympathy immediately flooded through her. "Oh, I'm so sorry," Erin said, wishing there were better words to convey the depth of the distress for him that she was feeling right at this moment.

She was well aware that losing someone close was like getting a punch to the stomach, one that refused to stop hurting. That was the way she'd felt when her father had died so suddenly, close to ten years ago. Her mother had been equally affected.

Erin knew that her mother had never gotten over it completely, despite the fact that the woman tried to behave as if she had moved on. She suspected that in a way it had to be the same for Steve and his son. And that Jason undoubtedly saw through his father's performance, just as she had seen through her mother's.

"And Jason's been playing that video game since he got it?"

Steve nodded. "Practically right from the beginning. Like I said, when he first started, I thought, 'Great, he's finally coming around, showing an interest in something. He's starting to play again.'

"The problem is he just plays the single-player version, so he's not playing against anyone. He still won't see any of his friends, no matter how many times I offer to invite them over. I've even passed by the school a few times when he was at recess. I'd see him sitting by himself in the schoolyard." He looked at Erin, shaking his head. Feeling completely helpless. "It breaks my heart but I don't know what to do."

Erin had a very basic question to put to him. "Have you tried talking to him?"

"Sure," he was quick to answer. "I talk to him all the time and once in a while, he nods in response or mumbles something, but for the most part, Jason lives in this world that I just can't reach."

Erin had a feeling that Steve misunderstood her question. She approached it from another angle. "Even when you talk to him about his mother?"

Steve didn't answer immediately. Instead, he took a moment to frame his reply. It didn't help. "Well, I don't— We don't— The subject isn't broached," he finally admitted.

"But the subject should be." Didn't he see that? The boy had lost his mother and he was obviously adrift because his father didn't seem to be missing her as much as he did. She could see that wasn't true, but she was a great deal older than just seven. "If you don't mind my butting in—"

"Please, butt in," Steve encouraged. At this point, he was willing to admit that he could use as much help as he could get.

"Okay, I think you need to help each other cope with this loss. The way I see it, Jason's playing that video game over and over again because in that universe, there's a chance he can control what's happening. In that universe, he wouldn't allow his mother to die—that's why he's slaying aliens constantly, to keep that world safe, and so, in a roundabout fashion, he's also keeping his mother safe."

Steve attempted to extrapolate from what she'd just said. "Then I shouldn't try to make him stop?" he asked uncertainly.

She had to be clearer, Erin scolded herself. "Oh, no, you definitely should. Jason needs to come back to the real world. He needs to be able to create safe places for himself. The way he can best do this is by using his imagination."

"In other words, he needs a Tex of his own."

Erin smiled and nodded. They were on the same page—finally. "Exactly."

Toy shopping was another thing that had been Julia's domain. In the past two years, he had been constantly realizing just how much he had abdicated to her, how much she'd actually been in charge of, relieving him of the burden. Now he had to take it all on as the different responsibilities and duties kept coming at him.

"You know, I'm pretty much a novice when it comes to toys. Where could I buy Tex?" Steve asked, adding, "I'm assuming that they're sold in stores, right?"

She smiled. "Actually, right now my stuffed animals are still mail order only, but the company is on the verge of being picked up by a couple of the larger toy-store chains." She didn't have to add that she was very excited about the pending prospect. It was evident in her voice.

At that moment, her cell phone began chiming in her purse. Digging it out, Erin shut off the alarm. She saw the curiosity in Steve's eyes.

"That's to remind me that I have a meeting in half an hour," she explained. Erin rose to her feet and he quickly did the same. "Tell you what—why don't you give me your card and I'll mail your son one of my toys."

"That would be great." Steve took out his wallet, extracted a business card and handed it to her. Then he opened his wallet to the section where he kept his bills. "How much do I owe you for the toy and for the shipping, of course?" he added as an afterthought.

"I'm not sure which toy I'm sending yet," she told him.

"Okay, then you'll include a bill inside the package." It was more of a confirmation than a question.

Erin vaguely nodded just as a second chime went off, reminding her to remember the reason for the first chime that had rung a few moments ago.

She flashed Steve an apologetic look. "It's a really important meeting," she told him. She glanced at his card as if to orient herself as to what was imprinted on it, then tucked it away. "Thank you for the coffee."

"Hey, thank *you* for the company—and the advice," he added.

"Then you'll talk to your son?" she asked. Her interest wasn't about to vanish the moment she left the café. When she got involved in something, she stayed involved until the matter was resolved. "About his mother?" she coaxed.

"I'll try," was all he could promise. Talking about Julia's death at any length was still incredibly hard for him. Most of the time, he dealt with the subject by *not* dealing with it. Pushing thoughts of his late wife aside until he could handle them.

That hadn't really happened yet, despite the fact that he had forced himself—temporarily—to venture into the dating circus.

About to take flight—she *hated* being late—Erin paused just before the café's front door and said, "Do more than try. *Do.*"

And with that, she quickly made her exit.

Chapter Five

There were times when Erin could swear that she hit the ground running the second she got out of bed in the morning. The only thing that actually changed from time to time was the speed with which she ran, and that was either top speed or *close* to top speed.

Today was one of those top-speed days even though she had allowed herself to take that break right after she gave her talk to the second graders. Or maybe *because* she had taken that break, since it had eaten into her so-called available time.

As she sat at her desk working, Erin smiled to herself. She had to admit that sitting in the café talking with Steve had been a very pleasant experience. Especially since she hadn't been trying to impress the man or make up her mind whether or not she wanted to commit to a second date—because having coffee with him didn't constitute a date at all—she'd felt relaxed and more like her true self.

For his part, Steve had certainly gotten her to open up more about herself than she usually did. But in hindsight, she supposed that was probably his expertise as a lawyer at work.

Lawyer.

As her fingers flew across her keyboard, she laughed softly under her breath. The man certainly didn't seem like any lawyer she'd ever heard about. He wasn't pushy, invasive or annoying.

Erin caught her bottom lip between her teeth. She supposed that wasn't fair, casting lawyers in that sort of light, but that was the only image of lawyers she'd been privy to.

Less daydreaming, more thinking.

At the moment, she was working on a new idea in the back of her mind while trying to get organized for a presentation to one of the two toy-store chains that had come up as possible distributors of her toy line. Engrossed in juggling several thoughts at the same time, Erin heard the door to her cubbyhole of an office open. Normally she'd hear an obligatory rap on the door before it was opened. Not that anyone stood on formality at Imagine That, but a token nod toward it was more or less the going behavior.

Hearing someone come in and assuming that it was probably either Rhonda or Mike, the two team members she interacted with most, she asked, "What do you think of a cuddly lawyer dinosaur?"

"I don't think you can create a cuddly lawyer, but

then, I wouldn't have thought a T. rex could be cuddly, either, and look how wrong I was about that."

The voice didn't belong to either Rhonda *or* Mike.

Startled, Erin's head jerked up in time for her to see her mother walking in, closing the door behind her. "Mom, what are you doing here?"

Eleanor O'Brien lifted her shoulders in a vague shrug and let them fall, just the same way her daughter might do in response to a question.

"If the mountain won't come to Mohammed, apparently Mohammed has to come to the mountain. So here I am."

"So now I'm a mountain?" Erin suddenly had a quick flashback to another conversation not that long ago. Remembering, she flushed. "I missed dinner last night, didn't I? I'm sorry."

Eleanor let the incident slide. "It wasn't very exciting. Besides, you had that speech to get ready for today," her mother said, handing her an excuse to use. However, Erin had a feeling she was far from home free. "So how did it go? Career Day," her mother prompted. "How did it go?"

Dumbfounded, Erin stared at her mother. She hadn't mentioned anything specific about her presentation, because she knew it would send her mother off on another tangent about children and the fact that Erin didn't have any.

"How did you know about Career Day?" she asked.

"I'm a mother. I know everything," Eleanor said, as if being all-knowing about her daughter's life was a given. "If you ever become one, you'll see that it just naturally comes with the territory."

A baby dig—and it hadn't even taken her mother five minutes. Unbelievable, Erin thought. The woman was a pro.

Erin's eyes narrowed as she regarded the person she loved more than anyone else on the face of the world—but who was also able to drive her crazy faster than anyone else on the planet.

"You interrogated Gypsy, didn't you?" she guessed, referring to her assistant.

"Not necessary," her mother informed her loftily. "I told you, I know everything."

Okay, she could play along. "Have it your way, Mom. If you know everything, then you should also know how it went."

True to form, her mother didn't back away from her claim. She went around it instead. "True, but I like hearing it firsthand from you—it makes it so much more personal that way," Eleanor told her with a broad smile. "Besides, you and I hardly ever get to talk," she added with just the right forlorn note.

Erin looked at her mother patiently. They had been through a lot together and her mother had been her rock during the whole drawn-out experience of her chemo treatments. There was no way she would ever lose her temper with her mother, but that didn't mean that she wasn't onto the woman's tricks.

"Then who's that on the phone with me five nights out of seven if not you?" Erin asked innocently.

"Don't get wise, Erin. I raised you better than that—and it's only four nights out of seven," Eleanor corrected her. "*If* I'm lucky."

Left unchecked, her mother could go on like this for hours. "Mom, I'm really very busy—"

"Yes, I know that, dear," Eleanor cut in. "And very successful, too. But someday, when I'm gone, you're going to regret not pausing once in a while to talk to me in person—but then it'll be too late."

All her mother was missing was a wrist dramatically laid across her forehead. Erin sighed, pushing herself back from her desk.

"Okay, okay, I give up. Talk," she declared, then added, "You know, Mom, you really should be giving guilt-wielding classes."

"I'm thinking about it, dear," Eleanor acknowledged with a weary smile. "It would be a way to fill up my empty hours—until I get a grandchild to play with, of course."

The woman never missed a chance, Erin thought. "Mom—"

Eleanor raised her hands at the warning note in her daughter's voice. "I'm backing off. Besides, you said you surrendered," she reminded Erin. "So we'll make it quick. Tell me about Career Day. Was Tex a hit?"

"He always is," Erin said proudly.

"You probably made it very difficult for someone to follow you," her mother theorized.

Erin looked at her sharply. "What are you talking about?"

Eleanor spread her hands wide. "Well, I'm assuming that you weren't the only one in the classroom talking about your career. They usually have at least two people, don't they?" she asked innocently.

Maybe she was just being unduly suspicious, Erin

thought. For now, she'd give her mother the benefit of the doubt—although her gut told her that there was more to all this than met the eye.

"You seem to have more experience with that than I do," Erin said, "but yes, as a matter of fact, there was someone else there, too."

"What did he do for a living?" Eleanor asked. Deliberately avoiding Erin's eyes, she picked up a small statue from her desk. It was of one of Erin's other creations.

Erin's radar had already gone off. "How did you know it was a he?" she asked.

"Fifty-fifty chance of being right," Eleanor replied sedately, still toying with the statue. "Mrs. Reyes probably wanted to give the boys an equal chance to relate to someone—not that *everyone* doesn't relate to you," she quickly added. "But at that age, guys like having a male authority figure to look up to."

"How did you know the name of the teacher?" Erin asked, then sighed, knowing her mother would continue to play it close to the vest. After all those years of being closer than most mothers and daughters, she knew it had to be twice as hard for her mother to let go and let her live her own life. While she sympathized with that, she was also determined to be her own person. "You either have a crystal ball—" Erin leveled a penetrating gaze at her mother "—or a spy."

Eleanor carefully put the little statue back, patting it on the head as she did so. "I told you, darling, I'm a mother. I know these things."

"Uh-huh." *No* one was that good at pulling facts out of the air. Besides, her mother looked much too innocent—which just meant that she had become far more devious than she usually was.

Eleanor got back to her previous question. "So what did this man you shared Career Day with do?"

Erin pulled her chair back up to her desk and began to type again. "About ten minutes."

"For a living, not how long he spoke," Eleanor emphasized.

Erin shrugged dismissively. "He's a lawyer."

Eleanor's whole countenance lit up. "And you wanted to immortalize him with a dinosaur? He must have created some impression on you for that," she cried enthusiastically. "What did he look like?"

Erin closed her eyes and sighed. She had really walked into that one. "I wasn't immortalizing him. It was just an idea for another toy, that's all."

It was Eleanor's turn to murmur "uh-huh" as if she didn't believe what she was hearing. "What did he look like?" she asked her daughter again.

Erin began to shrug again, then realized her mother would take that as a sign of nervousness or something equally as damning. She dropped the shoulder that had begun to rise.

"I didn't really notice. He was tall, dark haired with really green eyes and he was around thirty-three, maybe thirty-four."

Eleanor inclined her head, not bothering to hide her wide smile. "Not bad for not noticing."

She was not about to go down without a fight. "I have an eye for detail. Sue me."

"More lawyer talk," Eleanor enthused, her eyes

sparkling like her daughter's were capable of doing when she was caught up with something.

"Mother, you're hopeless!" Erin cried, bordering on exasperation.

Blessing Maizie silently in her head, Eleanor did her best not to come across as *too* eager as she asked, "So when are you seeing him again?"

"What do you mean, 'again'?" Erin stopped pretending to type—because at this point, her mind was *not* on her toys. Her mother's question indicated that she knew about the casual café stop. "How did you know?" she asked suspiciously.

Eleanor was instantly intrigued. "How did I know what?" Her enthusiasm was building by the moment. She was going to take Maizie out for the best meal of her life if this ended up with her daughter *finally* giving up her single status. "You've already seen him?"

Belatedly, she realized that her mother wasn't talking about the café—how could she be? Her mother was a great many things, but clairvoyant was not one of them.

"Well, yes, in the classroom," Erin said, doing her best to backtrack.

But it was too late to attempt to cover anything up. She could tell by looking at her mother's expression. Eleanor had always been extremely good at reading between the lines.

"That's not what you meant and you know it. Erin Sinead O'Brien, give me a little credit. I'm your mother. I know when you're not telling the truth."

There was no point in trying to deny it. Besides,

it was harmless, right? She was never going to see the man again.

Even so, Erin closed her eyes and sighed. "We just went out for coffee after we gave our talks. Please don't make a big deal out of it, Mom, because it wasn't."

"Erin, you haven't been out with a man in three years, not since you started up this company. Let me cherish this crumb for a brief moment."

She really didn't want her mother to get her hopes up—nothing was going to come of it.

"There's nothing to cherish, Mother. He's a very nice man who said he had a little extra time and wanted to know if I'd join him for a cup of coffee. When he mentioned French pastries, I decided why not? That's all there was to it. You're making too much of it."

Eleanor appeared not to hear her protest. Instead, she asked, "What's his name?"

"Why, so you can start sending out wedding invitations?" Erin challenged.

"So I'd know how to refer to him," Eleanor corrected, then grinned as she said, "but that sounds pretty good, too."

Erin felt as if she had one foot caught in the stirrup of a galloping horse. She had to find a way to stop her mother before someone got hurt—or trampled, she thought sarcastically.

"You don't need to know how to refer to him, Mom, because there's not going to be anything to refer to him about." Gritting her teeth, she went through it one more time. "He was just a nice man who got roped into giving a talk to his son's class, same as me."

Eleanor picked up on an important point. "So he has a son."

Too late Erin realized her slip. "Brilliant deduction, Mom. Will you *please* stop playing detective and trying to make this into something it's not?" she pleaded. "I've got a presentation to get ready."

"You're giving a speech in another classroom?" her mother asked hopefully.

Erin didn't even attempt a denial. Instead she just stated the fact as it was.

"A presentation to a representative of a toy-store chain." Maybe if she told her mother how important this was, she would cease and desist trying to pair her off with Jason's father. "I just need to impress *one* of these people and then Tex goes national." She looked at her mother earnestly. "Mom, this is really, really important to me. It's what we've been working toward for the last three years. If the toy chain likes us, this could be the difference in ultimately making it—or failing."

Eleanor rose from her seat and she smiled warmly at her daughter. She would have been proud of her no matter what she did and whether or not it was a success. The very fact that she was here at all was a miracle to her that she never took for granted. She wanted Erin to one day feel what she was feeling right now—overwhelming love for her child.

"Success is wonderful, Erin, but it doesn't keep you warm at night."

Erin gave her a wide, patient smile. "Oh, but it

does if you're successful enough to afford an electric blanket."

Eleanor laughed softly. "Okay, I give up—for now," she added, then asked, "Dinner next week?"

Right now, next week seemed light-years away. She would have agreed to almost anything just to be able to get her space back. She needed to get this presentation in top condition.

"Sure. Dinner. Next week. See you then, Mom."

Coming around the desk, Eleanor paused just long enough to press a kiss to her daughter's forehead. "Don't work yourself to death, darling. Just remember, you belong to me—until you get married."

"You make a persuasive argument for marriage," she quipped before beginning to type. "Goodbye, Mom." And then Erin glanced up one last time to add, "Sorry about last night."

Eleanor merely nodded. "You'll make it up to me," she said knowingly.

There was a strange promise in her mother's voice that Erin didn't catch until she played the words back in her mind a minute later. Erin looked up, but her mother had gone, closing the door behind her again.

Erin shrugged. Maybe it was just her imagination going into overtime. In any case, she didn't have time to try to figure out which it was and what her mother meant if it *was* some sort of promise. Right now she had a presentation to wrap up and that was all that really mattered.

It wasn't until the next day, after she, Rhonda and Mike—with Gypsy in tow for when it came time to display their sales stats—had gone before representatives of The Toy Factory to pitch a number of her best creations, that Erin felt relaxed. The representatives had all been sufficiently impressed and said that they would talk to the board members but that they were very optimistic that they had a deal.

A minor precelebration—she wasn't about to call it anything else until there was a contract for her to sign—was in swing when she remembered her promise from the day before. Not to her mother but to the man her mother had tried so hard to get her to talk about.

She'd promised Steve Kendall a replica of Tex for his son and she never broke a promise.

At least not intentionally, she amended, thinking of the dinner at her mother's that she'd forgotten about.

What if Steve had told his son that the stuffed animal was coming in the mail? If she'd mailed it yesterday, then the boy would be anticipating it to arrive today. Even if she expressed it in the next few minutes, there was no way that it would be there in time. Suddenly, she had an image of the slight boy with the curly blond hair standing next to his mailbox, watching as the mailman stuffed only letters into the box before driving off. There were times when there was such a thing as having *too* much imagination.

But that didn't change the fact that the package wouldn't get there today. She knew what it felt like to be disappointed. There was no way that she wanted to be the reason that a child experienced that feeling.

Erin made up her mind.

She looked around at the other people in the giant

room that served as the area where they brainstormed, created and manufactured the toys that were sold under the Imagine That banner. There were six people here, not counting her. Gypsy, her assistant, was also their go-to IT person. Rhonda and Mike were the ones who did most of the brainstorming with her while Judith, Neal and Christian took the drawings and made them into three-dimensional toys. They had become as much a part of her family as her mother was.

"Guys, I've got to go," she announced, trying to remember where she'd left her oversize purse.

"But you're the guest of honor—you can't leave," Christian protested.

"We'll have to stop partying," Gypsy said, pouting.

"No, you won't. You all worked hard," Erin told them. "You go right on partying. But I have a promise to keep."

"Right, dinner with your mother," Mike said, nodding his head. "You'd better go. You've already stood her up once this week."

Erin stared at him, only slightly dumbfounded. "Does everyone know every detail of my life?" she asked.

"What life, sweetness?" Christian teased. "You live here, remember? With us. All we'd need to do is put in a couple more hours a day and we'd be like that reality show where a whole bunch of people live together."

"Except that we have more class and we don't get on each other's nerves," Gypsy said brightly.

"Speak for yourself," Mike deadpanned. "Me, I'd

mow the lot of you down in an instant for box seats at a Dodgers game."

"He's kidding," Gypsy said with a nervous laugh, then looked at Erin as the latter began to leave. "He's kidding, right?"

Despite her uncanny ability when it came to computers, Gypsy had the innocence of a child at times. "Yes, he's kidding, aren't you, Mike?" Erin said pointedly.

Rail thin and dark haired, Mike saluted her. "Whatever you say, my liege."

"Maybe we should keep less long hours," Erin concluded.

"From your lips to God's ears, boss," Mike agreed, calling after her.

Erin merely waved her hand over her head to indicate that she'd heard. But she kept walking, knowing if she stopped even for a moment longer, chances were that she'd never get out.

And there was a little boy out there, waiting for a dinosaur.

Chapter Six

Erin parked next to the curb, turned off her engine and then took a deep breath as she gathered herself together.

This wasn't something she normally did, but then, the last couple of days had definitely been spent out of her comfort zone. First addressing a classroom of children, then pitching a partnership with a toy-store chain and now this personalized delivery service. Not exactly on the same level as slaying dragons, but still, for her, not something she was all that accustomed to.

But to not do this would somehow be breaking her word to a child, even if that word had been given through a third person.

Okay, let's do this and go.

Getting out of her vintage white Civic, Erin rounded the hood and went to the passenger side.

"Let's go, big fella," she said to the large stuffed dinosaur that had been riding shotgun over to Jason Kendall's home.

The plan was simple enough. She was going to put the Tex the T. rex toy on the front doorstep, ring the doorbell and leave. No explanations seemed necessary. All Jason needed to do was take one look at the dinosaur and her presence would have been superfluous.

She managed to get the putting-down part and the ringing-the-doorbell part right, but when she herself turned to quickly leave, the left heel of her stiletto got caught in a minor crack in the cement step that she hadn't even noticed until it took her shoe prisoner.

So instead of pivoting and going, she pivoted and suddenly found herself lunging forward because her left shoe, which sported laces up past her ankle, didn't go along with the momentum of the rest of her.

When the front door was opened in response to the doorbell, the person standing in the doorway found her in a crouching position on the front step. For a moment, the cheery-looking green dinosaur in the cowboy hat and holster went completely unnoticed.

"Erin?" Steve said quizzically, trying to make some sense of what he was looking at.

She looked at him over her shoulder. There was a chagrined expression on her face. "Sorry, I was just going to drop Tex off and go, but your front step seemed to have other ideas," she told him. "I think it wants to keep my shoe for a souvenir."

"Are you hurt?" was the first thing he asked.

"No, I have very resilient ankles," she said wryly,

wishing there were a way to just make herself disappear.

As if he was suddenly coming to, Steve quickly said, "Here, let me help you up."

Taking her hands, he drew Erin up to her feet. For a second he was acutely aware that her body seemed to be exceedingly close to his. There wasn't enough space between them for a vanilla wafer and he could feel a great many emotions he'd thought long dead and buried stirring within him, apparently very much alive.

Forcing himself to focus on *her* problem and not his, he looked down at her captive foot. The shoe still wasn't budging, so Steve bent down to the shoe's level to see what he could do. As he took hold of her ankle, he tried to pull her free of the crack.

Belatedly, he glanced up and asked, "You don't mind, do you?"

"Well, ordinarily I don't usually let a guy touch my ankle until the third date, but in this case, do what you have to," she cracked. When he seemed a wee bit puzzled, she shrugged. "Sorry, I tend to make jokes when I'm uncomfortable."

"Physically or emotionally?"

"Both." She was still stuck and growing more embarrassed by the second. "Maybe if I stepped out of the shoe," Erin suggested.

Since the shoes were laced up in the front, she started to bend down to loosen the laces. He beat her to it by undoing the bow at the top.

"I'll do it," he volunteered, then realized that she might not want him to. He had no idea what the right or wrong thing in this situation actually was. "Unless you have some objection to that."

"Why? It's a shoe, not a dress. Besides, I've always wanted to know what it felt like to be Cinderella in reverse."

She saw the question in his eyes. "You know, instead of trying on the glass slipper, the slipper's being taken off." Feeling really awkward, Erin blew out a breath. "Maybe I should just keep quiet. Talking isn't always my forte."

Steve laughed, shaking his head. "You sure could have fooled me," he told her. Glancing down at her shoe, he finished untying the laces. "Okay, I've taken your foot out of bondage."

Erin quickly slipped out of the trapped shoe. Standing unevenly on the step with one foot bare while the other was still wearing the four-inch heel, she watched as Steve gently rocked her shoe back and forth until he managed to free the heel out of the crack it'd been stuck in. Miraculously, the heel remained intact. She'd expected it to break in half.

"There you go," Steve declared, rising to his feet and offering her the shoe. "Good as new."

One hand on his shoulder to brace herself, Erin slipped her shoe back on. "Too bad the same can't be said about my pride."

"Wait," Steve said as she began to take a step. Crouching again, he started lacing up the shoe. "You don't want to trip on your laces," he told her, then got back to what she'd just said. "Why? What's wrong with your pride?"

He was just being nice, she thought, pretending not

to know. "I wasn't exactly the last word in gracefulness when you opened the door just now."

Finished, he rose again. "You weren't? I didn't notice a thing," he said, keeping a straight face. "Well, now that you're no longer a damsel in distress, why don't you come in for a few minutes?" he proposed, nodding toward the inside of his house.

She just wanted to slink away as fast as possible. "No, that's all right. I don't want to impose—"

But as she began to go, Steve caught her wrist, holding it lightly. "There's no one in the house except for Jason and me—and we're not imposable."

Was that even a word? She knew better than to ask. But even so, Erin still just wanted to leave the scene of her less-than-graceful interlude. "I just wanted to drop off Tex, like I promised."

"When you mentioned giving one to Jason yesterday, I thought you were going to mail it to him, not hand-deliver it."

"I *was* going to mail it," she explained. "But then I got caught up in getting ready for the presentation to the toy-store chain and I forgot all about sending a Tex plush toy to Jason," she admitted.

Frankly, he was surprised that she remembered the promise two minutes after she'd left the café. That she hadn't forgotten impressed him and had him looking at her in a very different, interested light.

"So you came by to deliver it in person?" he questioned incredulously.

The shrug seemed automatic. "I hate breaking promises to children."

"I was the one you told," he reminded her. "Not

Jason. Just what exactly is your cutoff point for the term *children?*" he asked, amused.

"Oh, no, I didn't mean to imply that I thought *you* were a child," she said quickly. As she continued, her momentum picked up with every word she uttered. She was all but breathless by the end. "It's just that I thought you might have told Jason and then if *he* was expecting to get Tex in the mail and nothing showed up, he'd be disappointed and—"

Now he really *was* impressed. "Wow, you really are one of a kind," he marveled. Steve picked up the dinosaur that was still standing there on the front step and practically pushed it into her hands. "Now you really have to hand this to Jason in person." As she began to demur, he told her, "Trust me, this is going to be one of those things that'll leave a huge impression on him when he looks back. And maybe, just maybe, getting this from you might manage to tear him away from that video game he won't stop playing."

Aware only of her parents' approach to child rearing, Erin asked him a very obvious question. "Have you tried to get him to stop playing?"

Did she think he was that much of a pushover? "I have."

"And?" she asked, her voice trailing off after uttering the single word.

"And Jason acts as if I've literally cut out his heart. He cries—not wild, tantrumlike screams but quiet, heartbreaking sobs." Steve sighed. Another father might have stuck to his guns, but he wasn't another father. He was the father of a seven-year-old who'd lost his mother and was trying to find his place in the world. "I wind up handing the game back to him, telling him it was okay. I know I should just put my foot down, but he's been through so much, I just don't want to add to that trauma even a little bit."

Steve shrugged helplessly, looking down at the stuffed animal she now had in her arms. "I guess I'm hoping that Tex can do what I can't. Separate Jason from his video game."

Touched, Erin nodded her head. She couldn't just leave after that. It just wouldn't be right. "If you put it that way, I guess I really can't say no—"

Steve grinned broadly. "I was really counting on that—now that you're here," he added.

Steve held the door open for her, then closed it behind them.

Erin stood in the foyer and looked around for a moment, getting her bearings. Directly in front of her was a long, winding staircase. On her right was what appeared to be a formal living room while the left led to what she took to be a family room.

She suddenly heard the loud sound of things breaking and falling. She looked toward Steve for some sort of an explanation.

He didn't have to look to know. The sound was more than familiar to him.

"That would be the latest batch of aliens dying by Jason's hand. He's gotten very good at wiping out eight-foot gray aliens. The universe should be safe for another day."

"I see. I guess I can buy some green bananas, then. They'll have a chance to ripen," she explained, flashing a smile at him that he found to be almost electrifying.

"Hey, buddy, there's someone here to see you," Steve called out to his son as they entered the family room.

As was his habit, Jason was in the room lying flat on his stomach, every fiber of his being focused on the action on the screen and what he was doing—eliminating the alien threat so that everyone he loved would be safe for another night.

The seven-year-old was so engrossed in the video game he barely grunted an acknowledgment to what his father had just said. It was obvious that he hadn't heard a single word, just the familiar drone of his father's voice.

Steve was about to tell Jason to shut off the game—Erin could just tell by his body language.

Instead she surprised him by placing a hand on *his* wrist to keep him from saying anything else or issuing any sort of an ultimatum to the boy.

The next moment, the voice of Tex the T. rex was heard saying, "Whatcha doin', Jason?"

Stunned, surprised, Jason instantly scrambled up off his stomach and temporarily forgot about his alien-killing mission. His eyes grew as large as the proverbial saucers when his suspicions turned out to be true. Tex was in his house, being held by the lady who had been to his classroom yesterday along with his father.

"You're the lady with Tex the T. rex," he cried in disbelief.

Erin grinned as she glanced in Steve's direction.

"Magna cum laude in my graduating class and I'm now 'the lady with Tex the T. rex,'" she said, shaking her head. But one look at her face told Steve she was both amused and pleased by the label—which, after all, was a kind of fame all its own.

"Yes, I am," she answered the boy. "I dropped by to bring you Tex Jr." She nodded at the stuffed toy she was holding.

"There's a Tex Jr.?" Jason asked her in wide-eyed surprise.

"There is indeed and he's here to keep you company." Erin held out the toy to him.

Jason took it rather tentatively. "I thought I was going to get Tex."

"Jason," Steve chided, embarrassed. "That's not what you say."

"It's okay," Erin assured him, then turned toward the boy. "I'm afraid I couldn't give him away," she told Jason solemnly. "Tex the T. rex is my very best friend. You wouldn't want me to give away my best friend, now, would you, Jason?" she asked.

Jason was quiet for a moment, as if he was actually pondering the question she had put to him. Then, with a huge sigh that seemed to reverberate throughout his small body, he said with a touch of resignation, "No, I guess not." Then he looked down at the stuffed dinosaur he *was* holding. "But it's okay to give Tex Jr. away?" he asked.

The boy had a sharp mind, she thought. "Well, not just away to anyone, mind you," she said as seriously as if she were having a conversation with an adult about this. "I mean, it has to be someone special. Someone who's going to promise not to let Tex Jr. get too lonely and start missing his dad."

She pretended to regard Jason for a long moment, as if assessing whether or not he could live up to his responsibilities.

"Think you're up to doing that?" she asked. Jason bobbed his head up and down even as she continued. "That means that you have to be there for him any time he needs you." When he nodded again, she pretended to cup her ear as if to pick up any stray sound. "I can't hear you," she said in her best drill-sergeant voice.

"Yes, I can!" Jason declared with enthusiasm.

Erin nodded, as if he had finally managed to convince her. "Okay, then Tex Jr. is all yours. Remember to always love him and be there for him."

"I will." He looked down at the plush toy in his arms. "Hi, I'm Jason. I'm your new friend," he told the dinosaur. "What do you wanna do first?" When he received no response from the toy, he looked up at Erin, confused. "How come he doesn't talk?" he asked.

"Well, that's really all up to you and your imagination," she told the boy.

"Me?" he asked, puzzled. "How?"

"You're the one who has to put the words in his mouth. Just like I'm the one who puts words into Tex Sr.'s mouth."

The revelation seemed to only confuse Jason more.

Steve wanted to step in with an explanation of his own, but he was curious to see how this energetic dynamo was going to handle it, so he kept quiet.

"You make Tex talk?" Jason asked in wonder.

Erin nodded. "Yes, I do."

Convinced that she was teasing him, Jason protested adamantly, "No, you don't. You're making that up," he insisted. "Tex doesn't sound like you and I don't see your mouth move when he talks."

"That's because she's a ventriloquist," Steve told his son, coming to her rescue.

"A what-o-quist?" the boy asked, his small eyebrows puckered into a wavy, quizzical line.

"Ventriloquist," Erin repeated, then explained, "It means someone who throws their voice."

Jason looked more confused than ever as he looked from the woman who had given him the very silent Tex Jr. to his father, who had never lied to him before.

"I don't get it. How can anyone throw a voice?" he asked, and then brightened. "Is it like throwing a ball?"

"Maybe," she agreed, trying to figure out how to make the analogy work for the boy. "It's like throwing an invisible ball and making it land right in front of who you *think* you're talking to."

Jason frowned. "Prove it," he said. "Make him say my name, sounding like big Tex," he requested.

Well, at least that was easy enough, Erin thought.

"Hi, I'm Tex Sr., Jason," his new stuffed toy said. "And I'm too old for these silly games. I just like smart games—like jumping out airplanes and big, brave stuff like that."

Erin frowned and gave the dinosaur a long reproving look. She blew out a breath, then asked sternly, "Tex, what did we say?"

The smaller version of her first stuffed dinosaur suddenly hung its head.

"You said not to brag." And then the toy's head bobbed up. "But I wasn't bragging. I was just saying it like it was."

"Tex." She drew out his name like a mother calling her child out on the carpet because he'd just told a lie.

There was a loud huff of a sigh. "Okay, okay, I was saying it like it wasn't. Can't a guy have a little fun around here? Huh? Can't he? Can't he?"

Erin arched one eyebrow as she looked down at the toy. "If you ask me, you're having a little too much fun, Tex."

"Ha!" That was when the dinosaur raised his little green chin. "There's no such thing as too much fun—right, Jason?" he asked, turning toward the boy. "C'mon, boy, back me up here."

Jason giggled, very pleased to be drawn into this new game. "Right!" he declared with enthusiasm.

"Okay, now you see how it's done?" Erin asked the little boy as she handed the toy back to him.

Jason inclined his head, willingly conceding the point. But he was also aware of what he viewed as an obvious problem.

"But I can't do it like you. My lips move when I talk," Jason protested.

"That's okay. There's absolutely nothing wrong with that," Erin assured him. "As long as you hear Tex Jr. saying the words in your imagination, it's the same thing and that's really all that counts. You see, the point is to use your imagination, Jason," she told him with emphasis. To underscore her point, she tapped his forehead lightly with her forefinger.

"Is that where my imagination is?" Jason asked, touching where Tex's friend had just tapped his forehead. "Right there? Inside my head?" he specified, doing his best to look serious.

"Right there," she confirmed. "In your mind. All you have to do is tap into it." Leaning over so that her lips were close to Jason's ear, she whispered, "Think about it and it will be."

Erin drew away to see if her words had made the right impression.

The boy's eyes were sparkling, as if he had just been given the secret of life.

"Really?" he asked in a hushed, almost worshipful voice.

"Really," she repeated with solemnity.

"Wow." Jason's smile was wide, excited and close to heart melting as he hugged his new toy to him and said to Erin, his voice muffled against the green plush material, "Thank you!"

"You are very welcome, Jason," she responded. "My pleasure entirely."

Out of the corner of her eye, she saw Steve beaming at her, a father grateful to her for what she'd just done for his son.

Something very warm and enveloping stirred within her.

Chapter Seven

Watching his son from across the room, Steve's arms were folded in front of his chest as if that stoic pose could somehow help him absorb what had just transpired before him.

When Erin came to join him, Steve lowered his voice and confided, "You know, this really is somewhat awe-inspiring."

Erin wasn't quite sure she was following him. "What is?" she asked in the same low whisper that he'd just used.

He didn't answer immediately. Just for the slightest moment, with Erin whispering back to him like that, it almost felt as if they were sharing some sort of intimate secret instead of what turned out to be an observation he was making.

The next moment, he pushed the feeling aside.

"I think I've just witnessed my first miracle," Steve told her, silently giving her all the credit for bringing the miracle about. "I didn't think anything but school and a strictly enforced bedtime could separate Jason from that infernal video game of his." He shook his head as he glanced toward the frozen screen—Jason had paused the game and the bottom of the monitor appeared to be littered with no-longer-functioning aliens. "He's been playing it for more than the last eighteen months. I was beginning to hear those aliens making that awful noise as they were being decimated in my sleep."

She could see that Steve was relieved—but she didn't want him getting carried away or thinking that the video game's reign was permanently over. Because it just might not be.

"It's not exactly a magic solution," Erin cautioned him, "but maybe it's actually a good start."

The woman was definitely a great deal less self-absorbed than any of the women he'd gone out with in the past few months. In his book, that made her far more genuine.

Maybe if one of the women he'd dated had been more like her, he wouldn't have sworn off dating.

"There's such a thing as undue modesty," he told her. "I just want you to know that you and Tex saved not one but two lives today."

She glanced back at the boy, then looked at Steve, confused. "Two?"

"Yes, my son—and my sanity. Technically, that would mean me, so you saved my life, as well. I really didn't know how much more I could take," he admitted now that there had been this breakthrough. "Jason used to be a happy, outgoing kid, but after Julia died—and especially since he started playing that video game—he became very isolated in that world of his."

She watched the boy as he played with the dinosaur. He was mirroring actions she'd witnessed in the test playgroups she'd conducted. Tex had sparked the boy's imagination. That was an exceptionally hopeful sign.

"Like I said, it's a start. I'm not an expert," Erin prefaced, choosing her words carefully. And then Steve interrupted her.

"You are in my book," he interjected. "You've certainly achieved more in a small space of time than I or Mrs. Malone, his sitter, have in the past eighteen months or so."

Erin started again. "I'm *not* an expert, but I'm pretty sure there will be some backsliding for Jason, so be prepared for it. That doesn't mean he'll go back to wrapping himself up in that video game and being uncommunicative and shutting you out. It just means that he'll be looking to find just where he belongs in this world where he can no longer see his mother. It's rough going, but I get the feeling that it'll wind up being okay."

Rather than view the possibilities negatively, Steve appeared to be genuinely impressed with what she was telling him.

"So tell me," he began, "did you take child psychology along with creative toymaking?"

"No, but for a few years back there, I was a child," she told him brightly. "And fortunately for my target audience, I am blessed with a *very* good memory. I can remember a *lot* of the things I felt back then as if they had all happened yesterday." Never one to try to call attention to herself or take too much credit, Erin paused and gave him a shy smile. "What that also means is that I would be pretty awful at disciplining kids because I'd remember just how it felt to be in their shoes and that would make me automatically give them a pass."

Steve read between the lines. "Then you don't have any kids of your own?"

She shook her head and tried not to visualize her mother's very disappointed expression as she said, "Nope, I'm afraid that I've never been lucky enough to have children."

He supposed it was wrong to push the envelope a little further, especially considering what she'd just done for his son—and him—but something more than just idle curiosity had him asking Erin, "But you *have* been married."

Erin shook her head again. "I took a pass on that, too. I was stuck in the hospital for over two years and when one day the doctors pronounced me cured, I couldn't wait to get back to actually living my life and *doing* things.

"It always felt as if I was running way behind the pack, trying desperately to catch up on everything I'd missed. Trying to make my life count for something." Erin flushed a little, feeling as if she was talking too much but wanting this man to understand where she was coming from. Understand where she'd been.

"I felt I had to prove to God that He did the right

thing saving me. And I guess what happened was that I was so busy trying to amount to something, to make a difference, that I forgot to pay attention to what was an important part of my life—or so my mother keeps telling me," she concluded with a grin.

"Let me guess. She's after you to get married, settle down and start a family, right?"

Erin laughed. It was her turn to be impressed. "Good guess. I take it you know my mother?" she asked, only half kidding.

"No, but I've got one of those, too. A mother," he explained in case she'd missed his meaning. "My mother was absolutely thrilled to death when Jason was born and, to give her credit, she was almost as devastated as I was when Julia died." And then he thought that perhaps he'd failed to tell Erin his wife's name. "Julia was my—"

"Wife," Erin supplied nodding her head. "Yes, I picked up on that yesterday," she told him sympathetically. "So has your mother begun dropping hints that maybe you should get married again?" she asked, fairly certain that she knew the answer to that.

Steve laughed. It was almost as if Erin had been looking into his life through a one-way glass.

"My mother doesn't really understand the word *hint*. She's more of the 'let's rent a billboard to catch his attention' type. She definitely does *not* beat around the bush," he added. "She was very gung ho about my getting back into the dating game." Now that he thought about it, his mother had been the one to all but talk him into it. She'd thought it was a good idea for Jason's sake.

"So you're dating," Erin concluded.

"No," he corrected her. "I *was* dating."

A man stopped dating for one of two reasons. Either he found the whole venture frustrating—and looking at him, she doubted that would have been the outcome—or he'd found someone to get serious about.

"Why the past tense?" she asked, feeling that perhaps he was just waiting for her to give him a verbal nudge so that he would give her the rest of the story.

Steve shrugged carelessly. "I found it just wasn't for me. I'm not really comfortable with the whole 'Am I impressing you enough?' ritual," he confided. "Besides, I found that the single women I dated weren't looking to get into a relationship with a man who has a child."

He knew that there had to be someone out there who would take Jason and him as a set, but for the moment, he'd decided just to take an extended break before getting back into that rat race. A very *long* extended break.

She kept watching Steve with a questioning look in her eyes. "Oh?"

He merely nodded. Truth be told, he was relieved to be taking this hiatus. There was just way too much pressure involved in dating.

"Yeah."

"And why do you think that is?" Erin asked, curious as to his reasoning as well as just what sort of women he had encountered to sour him this way on the whole concept of dating.

"Well, for one thing, I think the more intelligent

ones realized that because I had a son, it meant that they wouldn't always be first. To be very honest, I don't mind saying that my son is my first priority."

"As it should be," Erin agreed.

Her comment had him pausing for a second, surprised and impressed that she felt that way. He took the remark to be genuine since she apparently had nothing to gain by saying it.

"We've both gone through a lot," he continued, "but for him the impact is almost greater because he lost his mother. Somewhere in that head of his, I think he's afraid that something might happen to me and then he'll be all alone. I mean, there's my mother, but he's not as close to her as he was to Julia and me—or at least, he *used* to be to me." Steve looked at her. "With any luck, thanks to you and that dinosaur of yours, I've got a really good shot at getting my son back."

"He's always been yours, Steve. He just took a short hiatus," she told him knowingly. "But you know, you have to think ahead, too."

He wasn't sure where she was going with this. "What do you mean?"

"Well, right now it's you and Jason against the world, which is very sweet. But someday, say in about eight, nine years, he's going to want to break out of that cocooned universe you two have and explore a universe of his own, maybe try it on for size. He might even feel guilty about leaving you behind, but odds are pretty good that it's going to happen. Then you'll still be in that universe for two that you two currently have—except that you'll be the only one in it."

He looked at her, taken aback by what she was saying. "Wait, are you telling me to date?"

She raised her hand to stop his assumption before he got carried away in the wrong direction. "I'm not advocating it or putting a taboo on it," she told him. "I'm just saying you should consider all possibilities carefully—and more than once—before discarding them."

Even as the words came out, Erin realized that she sounded a little preachy. "But hey, what do I know?" she asked, not wanting him to think that she was lecturing him. "I'm a grown woman talking to stuffed green dinosaurs—and answering myself back in high voices."

That hadn't come out the way she'd intended. Maybe it was time for her just to leave before she said something else equally inane. The man probably thought she was a little strange at best, she reasoned.

Embarrassed, she felt a quick exit was her best bet. Much as she enjoyed watching the boy play with his new toy, it was time to leave.

"Look," she began awkwardly, "I've taken up your time long enough. I should let you get back to your evening and your son."

"This *is* my evening," Steve pointed out. "Until you showed up with Tex Jr. there, my evening was going to be sending out for pizza and then watching Jason slay more aliens and save the world for the umpteenth time. The way I see it," he told her, "for bringing peace into my world, I at least owe you dinner."

"Pizza?" she asked skeptically.

"Hey, it doesn't have to be pizza," Steve pointed out, warming up to the idea of having her stay a while longer. "There're a lot of takeout restaurants in the area. You can have your choice of cuisines and cultures—just name it."

Steve beckoned her over toward his kitchen. Once there he opened his "everything" drawer and began taking out the various folded menus he'd picked up and thrown in there.

"Thai food, Chinese, Mexican, Indian—whatever your pleasure, I most likely have a takeout menu to fit your appetite."

Erin looked at him, amusement taking hold. "What about home cooked?" she proposed.

"Home cooked," he repeated, looking through his selection. "That would be Marie Callender's," Steve concluded. He opened up another drawer. "Got the menu here somewhere," he told her, searching.

"No, as in *real* home cooking. From your home," she emphasized.

He certainly had the kitchen for it, she thought, looking around. It appeared to be the last word in gourmet cooking, from its overhead shiny pots hanging on hooks from the ceiling to its six-burner stove and wide counters.

He laughed and shook his head. "No, I had to take an oath that I would never attempt to do anything that involved an open flame and pots and pans."

"An oath to who?" she asked, curious as well as more than a little amused by his claim.

"To the fire department and the E.R. staff at the local hospital," Steve said in a perfectly serious voice.

"You're that bad, huh?" she asked, trying not to laugh.

There was absolutely no point in denying it. "Actually, I don't think they've invented the words to describe exactly how badly my culinary attempts have turned out. It's a really dark place. Better not to go there," he assured her.

"This ban on bringing your stove and the foodstuffs in your refrigerator together—does that just apply to you, or does everyone who comes into your house have to abide by it?"

"Well, a couple of Fridays ago, Cecilia did make dinner for Jason and me," he said, recalling the way the woman had just taken charge.

"Cecilia," Erin repeated, trying not to sound disappointed. "Then you are dating."

He grinned broadly. He wondered if Cecilia would have been insulted or amused if she'd heard what Erin had just said.

"Cecilia owns the house-cleaning company that keeps my house in the orderly condition you see— I'm not exactly much at cleaning, either," he confided. "Cecilia herself is a wonderful, wonderful woman, but she's around my mother's age. I don't think she's interested in going out with someone my age."

Erin felt a wave of relief and tried not to really take note of it. She was offering to cook for the man. It was strictly a harmless endeavor. Didn't mean anything, she told herself.

"Mind if I take a look in your refrigerator?" she asked him.

"Not much to see," he warned her even as he waved her over to it.

Erin took her own inventory quickly enough. "Eggs, milk, margarine," she noted, then opened the freezer door. "Frozen mixed vegetables." She glanced at him over her shoulder. This wasn't half-bad. "Not nearly as bare as I thought it would be."

Another careless shrug accompanied his words. "Well, in an emergency, I can make scrambled eggs if we're snowed in."

Amusement made it hard not to grin at his statement. "This is Southern California. The only snow you'd find around here is up at Big Bear—in the dead of winter—and you have to go to it, not it to you."

"My point exactly. I haven't had to break any eggs in a very long time."

Erin frowned, taking a second look at the carton that was in the refrigerator. She didn't detect any telltale smell of rotten eggs, but then, she still hadn't taken out the carton and opened it.

Glancing at him over her shoulder, she asked, "Exactly how old are these eggs?"

"I know what you're thinking," he told her. "Don't worry. Cecilia had one of her cleaning ladies pick up the carton the last time she was here. She said I should keep them and the rest of the groceries you see in the refrigerator around just in case. Oh, and the milk, by the way, is fresh. It goes with Jason's cereal. I do know how to open a box of cereal."

She grinned. "Good for you," Erin quipped. She eyed the various items her hunt had yielded and made her decision. "Okay, where do you keep your frying pan? Or did the fire department confiscate that from you as a precautionary measure, too?"

He opened up one of the cabinets and took out the pan for her, then placed it on the stove. "No, but I promised not to use it and my word was good enough for them," he deadpanned.

"Well, you'll be keeping your word to them—I'll be the one doing the cooking."

One of the things he'd picked up on during his brief venture into the dating realm was that most professional women had no time—or desire—to learn how to cook. He'd just naturally assumed that Erin was like the rest in that aspect.

"Didn't you say that you were too busy trying to catch up on everything you'd missed out on doing because you were in the hospital?"

"Yes, and cooking was one of those things." She laughed. "A creative person has to have more than one outlet in order to feel fulfilled and on top of their game. Me, I come up with some of my best ideas cooking. Cooking relaxes me," she explained.

"Funny, it has just the opposite effect on me," he said.

"Your strengths obviously lie in other directions," she countered.

Steve had to admit he appreciated the way she tried to spare his ego.

He watched Erin as she practically whirled through

his kitchen, getting unlikely ingredients out of his pantry and his cupboard. She assembled everything on the counter within easy reach, then really got busy as she began making dinner.

He had never been one who enjoyed being kept in the dark. "If you don't mind my asking, exactly what do you plan on making?"

"A frittata," she said cheerfully. Combining a total of eight eggs in a large bowl, she tossed in a dash of salt and pepper before going on to add two packages of the frozen mixed vegetables. She would have preferred to use fresh vegetables, but beggars couldn't afford to be choosers.

"A what?"

In another pan, she'd quickly diced up some of the ham she'd found as well as a few slices of cheddar cheese from the same lower bin drawer in the refrigerator.

She was about to repeat the word, then realized that it wasn't that Steve hadn't heard her—the problem was that he didn't know what she was referring to.

Opening the pantry again, she searched for a container of herbs or spices. There were none. She pushed on anyway, adding everything into the bowl with the eggs.

"Just think of it as an upgraded omelet. You have ham and bread," she said, pleased.

"That's because I also know how to make a sandwich without setting off the smoke alarm," he told her.

"There is hope for you yet," she declared with a laugh.

Watching her move around his kitchen as if she belonged there, he was beginning to think the same thing himself—but for a very different reason.

Chapter Eight

"What is this?" Jason asked between bites.

They—including Tex Jr. because Jason had asked for his new friend to be given a chair, as well—were all seated around the dining room table, eating Erin's creation.

"Jason, what did I say about talking with your mouth full?" Steve reminded him.

"Not to," Jason said dutifully, "but the food's not going to fall out. I got my chin up," he argued.

Erin didn't bother trying not to laugh. "I think his lawyer genes are showing up early," she told Steve. Turning toward the boy, she answered his initial question. "It's a frittata."

Erin noted, with no small pleasure, that Jason was making short work of her creation. She'd given him what she judged to be a decent-size portion for a seven-year-old. There were about two forkfuls left. He'd been inhaling it.

As had, she realized, his father. While the latter might have felt obligated to make a show of enjoying her spur-of-the-moment impromptu meal, she'd learned that children were far more honest in their dealings. If Jason hadn't liked it, he would have indicated as much, even if he hadn't given voice to his disdain.

Instead he was devouring it.

"A fri-what-a?" Jason asked, clearly having trouble wrapping his tongue around the word.

"A frittata," she repeated, then suggested helpfully, "How about we call it an omelet with everything?"

"Okay." Jason was quick to agree, bobbing his head up and down for added emphasis. "I like this," he told his father.

Erin had always had trouble accepting compliments and had always been quick to downplay any credit sent her way. "It's probably the ham," she told Steve.

"Funny, I was going to guess that it was probably the cook," Steve told her. "This really *is* good," he said, adding his voice to his son's praise. "I'd ask you to write down what you did, but like I said, there's a restraining order to keep me from getting within a hundred yards of the stove when it's turned on, so even if I had your directions, there wouldn't be anything I could do about it."

Her eyes met his. "Then how would you be able to make those scrambled eggs in an emergency as you'd mentioned?" she asked innocently.

She had him there, he thought. "Good one. I'll have to get back to you on that," he said. "In the meantime, feel free to come by anytime to work that magic on my stove—" he glanced toward Jason, who was busy "feeding" his new friend "—and my son."

That caught Jason's attention. His head swung around in her direction and just like that, she had his undivided attention.

"You do magic?" Jason asked, wide-eyed.

"No, I don't do magic," she said to the boy. "Your dad's just kidding."

He appeared disappointed for exactly five seconds. "Oh. But he's not kidding about you coming back, right?" Jason asked her, his eyes all but pinning her in place. "You will come back, right?"

"Would you like that, Jason?" Steve asked his son before Erin had a chance to say anything in response to the boy's question.

"Yes!" Jason declared with more enthusiasm than Steve had seen his son display in two years.

Steve smiled at him even as he slanted a glance toward the woman who in his opinion was solely responsible for the boy's transformation.

"Me, too," he told Jason. And then he looked at Erin. "Well, I guess that makes it unanimous. You're officially invited back to our house anytime—even if you don't feel like whipping up a frittata," he added with a smile. He didn't want her getting the mistaken idea that her main allure was that she seemed to know her way around the kitchen.

"And when you come back, you can bring Tex with you," Jason told her.

Erin cocked her head, looking at the boy. "So my return is a done deal?"

"Yeah!" And then the wide smile on his face drooped a bit around the corners as Jason struggled to understand the meaning behind her question. "Don't you wanna come back?"

Instead of immediately answering, she glanced at Steve, arching an eyebrow and waiting to see what he would say about the matter, one way or the other. She didn't want to presume too much. That was how people fell flat on their faces.

"Hey, I'm with him," he said, throwing his vote in with his son's.

Maybe she should be just a little clearer about this, Erin thought. "Well, I'll come back if I'm invited."

"You're invited. Right, Dad? She's invited," Jason declared, looking at his father expectantly, waiting for backup.

"That depends on whether or not she'd like to come back," he told his son. "But as far as I'm concerned, yes, she's invited. How about you, Tex Jr.? You want to tell us how you feel about having Erin come back for another visit?"

"I want her to come back for another visit right away!" Jason said in his best high-pitched voice as he pretended to be Tex Jr.

Steve let go of the breath he'd been holding. Her experiment in bringing the stuffed dinosaur into the boy's life to separate Jason from his gaming console had been a huge success in his book. His son was even imitating the way Erin had told him to act as the toy's voice.

Turning toward Erin, he said, "Looks like it's three against one."

"Three against one?" she repeated, looking from Steve to his son to the dinosaur. "Who said I didn't want to come back?" Erin asked. "Especially when you clean your plates like that."

"I can clean it even better with my tongue," Jason volunteered excitedly. Taking his plate in both hands, he was about to raise it to his mouth to give her a demonstration when Steve intervened, confiscating the plate.

"I think we'll just let the dishwasher take care of that," he said.

"Sounds like a very good idea," Erin said, backing him up.

"Oh. Okay," Jason agreed, then gave Erin a great big smile.

"The next time I come, I'll bring my own groceries," she promised Jason. "We'll make frittata with chicken." Leaning into the boy, she lowered her voice and pretended to confide, "Tex'll probably like it better."

He slanted a glance toward the dinosaur seated beside him. "Tex likes chicken?" he asked her.

She nodded. "T. rexes were carnivores," she told him. "That means that they liked to eat meat."

"They did?" Jason asked, fascinated as he absorbed every word she was saying to him.

Erin nodded her head, looking at him very solemnly. "Absolutely."

"Did you see them doing it?" he asked in a hushed voice. "Was it gross?"

"It was probably very gross," Erin said. To her credit, she kept a straight face. "But I didn't see them do it. However, lots of paleontologists did a great deal of research about our dinosaur friends and they've put together a lot of books describing what the dinosaurs were like."

Jason looked as if he was struggling not to be completely confused by the information.

"What's a pale—a pale—one of those people you just said?" he finally asked.

"Paleontologists are people who study things that happened a very long time ago," she explained.

Pausing for a moment, she crossed to where she'd dropped off her purse and fished out the book she'd brought with her. When Steve had discovered her on the doorstep before she could successfully make her getaway, struggling to retrieve her shoe, she'd forgotten all about the book she had brought with her. The book, which she'd originally written, was packaged with every junior T. rex that was sent out of the factory.

"Here, you can read all about what the T. rex was like when he roamed the Earth and was the undisputed king of all that he saw."

Jason, in Steve's opinion, looked as if he were back in wonderland again, hanging on every word that came out of this woman's mouth. If he were being completely honest, Steve thought, he was beginning to find her pretty fascinating himself.

"That's for me?" Jason asked, surprised even as he held the colorful book in both hands.

"I brought it just for you," Erin said, fully enjoying his reaction. She'd channeled the little girl she had been when she was writing this book and she knew for a fact that children enjoyed reading it, but once in a while, it was nice to be able to witness that joy firsthand. "Reading about things is still the best way to learn and remember," she told the little boy.

Shifting the book to just one hand, he picked up the T. rex with his other hand and tucked the stuffed dinosaur against him. "C'mon, Tex Jr., let's find out all about you."

"Okay," the stuffed animal answered in Jason's high-pitched voice.

If he weren't afraid that it might freak Erin out, he would have hugged her, Steve thought. His exuberance had risen to that level.

"You really *are* a magician," Steve said. "No ifs, ands or buts about it. Jason and that infernal video game have now been separated for—" he glanced at his watch to verify his findings "—close to an hour. That's a new world record for him."

Erin didn't think she deserved all that much credit. "Very few boys his age can resist dinosaurs. All I did was bring the two together."

Steve shook his head. "There's that undue modesty again."

Seeing that the man seemed really determined to give her credit for his son's about-face, she decided she was fighting a losing battle.

"I didn't do anything that special, but have it your way," she said, surrendering.

Steve grinned at her. "Like I said, you are a *rare* woman."

If she wasn't careful, all this flattery was going to go to her head. Thank God she had a crew to keep her grounded, although it was kind of nice to bask in adulation for a couple of minutes.

However, she wasn't sure just what Steve was referring to by declaring her to be unique amid her gender.

"How's that again?" she asked him.

"I haven't encountered a woman recently who willingly told me to have it my way—about anything," Steve was quick to add, in case she thought he might be referring to something strictly sexual.

"I find that really hard to believe."

Her response caught him up short. "Oh? Why?"

"Well, for one thing, you're a lawyer. Aren't all lawyers supposed to wear the opposition down until they agree with you?" And then she thought of the one possible exception to that. "Unless, of course, you've been socializing with other lawyers. Then, of course, the back-and-forth arguing could literally go on for hours, I imagine." And that made her think of something else. "By the way, did I tell you I'm considering a new character in my dinosaur lineup? I'm thinking of calling him Clarence Darrow-Dinosaur," she told him.

Trying to keep up with her was definitely a challenge. The woman had a mind that insisted on jumping from topic to topic. "Clarence Darrow-Dinosaur?" he repeated.

She'd just thought of the name as she told Steve about this new character. "I thought I'd give the kids a double blast of history this time around, have a small biography of Clarence Darrow in the accompanying book as well as some background on whatever dinosaur I decide to make Clarence." Chewing on her bottom lip, she looked up at him. "Any suggestions?"

It wasn't as if he had a favorite dinosaur he wanted to lobby for, although watching Jason play with his new best friend had suddenly made him rather partial to a T. rex. "I'm fine with any kind you want— except for a raptor," he qualified. When he'd been a kid, he'd seen them vividly portrayed in a movie and the vicious image had stayed with him for years. "They really do give me the creeps."

"Got it. No raptor. What about a brachiosaur?" she suggested. "They're *not* flesh eaters," she added when his expression remained blank.

The one piece of information did the trick. "They get my vote," he said.

"Brachiosaur it is, then," she said, finalizing the decision.

Erin glanced over into the family room and saw that Jason was apparently giving his new friend a tour of the room and explaining things. She'd united the boy with his dinosaur and fed both him and his father. Her work here was more than done. Time to retreat into the sunset.

"Well, I really better be going or I am going to be horribly behind by tomorrow morning," she told Steve.

"You do sleep, right?" Steve asked. He was disappointed to see her leave so soon, but he knew he had no right to monopolize this woman, especially after everything she'd done.

"Sometimes, if I'm not too far behind."

Although, more accurately, there were times when she got only a couple of hours at best. She felt as if there was so much she still needed to make up for and catch up on. The two years she'd spent in the hospital felt like two decades at times.

"Just remember, it's good to slow down once in a while," he told her. "Burning the candle at both ends does catch up to you eventually."

My God, had he been talking to her mother? Erin wondered. The next moment, she dismissed the idea since even she hadn't known she was going to be spending time here at his house. There was no way her mother could have known that and given him a pep talk.

"I've got a ways to go before that happens," she assured him.

"You'd be the best judge of that," he agreed. Well, since she was determined to leave, the least he could do was escort her out. "Here, let me walk you to your car," he offered.

"That's not necessary," she demurred. "Besides, you don't want to leave Jason alone."

He glanced over his shoulder toward where his son was. Not in his customary pose—lying flat on his stomach and looking straight ahead at the TV screen, glassy-eyed, mowing down aliens—the boy was sitting upright on the family room floor talking to the toy Erin had brought to him.

"Jason's not alone, thanks to you," Steve pointed out. "And I'm assuming that you didn't park in the next development, so it's not like I'm going off on this tremendous hike."

"No," she agreed. "I parked my car right at your front curb."

That was what he'd thought. Steve nodded at her response. "I think that Jason and Tex Jr. can spare me for twenty feet."

He walked her to his front door, opened it for her, then waited as she crossed the threshold. Once she had, he followed closely behind. He left the door opened behind him in case Jason came looking for them—or him.

But right now the focus of his attention was the petite woman next to him. "I'd like to thank you for going out of your way like that for Jason. I really appreciate your effort."

She could feel color preparing to creep up her neck. Direct compliments, even simple ones honestly rendered, embarrassed her to no end. She didn't know what to do with her hands, where to look. What to do with her face. Was she supposed to look gratified, humbled, or what exactly?

So she fell back on what she usually did under these circumstances. She shrugged the words off. "It was nothing."

But Steve—or his words, she was beginning to realize—was not that easy to shrug off.

"No, it most definitely was something," the lawyer insisted. "And I owe you. Big-time." In keeping with what had become a magical evening, he offered, "One free wish of your choosing."

Humor curved her mouth and then moved up into her eyes, making them sparkle.

"You belong to the genie union?" she asked.

"Hey, if you can bring my son a dinosaur in a cowboy hat and suddenly wind up tapped into his imagination—something that I was becoming convinced had deserted him—then I can make at least one wish come true for you," he informed her.

"Wouldn't that depend on the kind of wish I make?"

Steve nodded. "It would."

He still didn't see it, she thought. She could tell by the look in his eyes. So she tried to make it clearer for him. "So I'd better not wish for anything outlandish," she surmised.

"One man's outlandish is another man's mundane."

He was better at this than she'd thought, Erin realized, tickled. The man had potential. Not only that, but try as she might not to, she could see herself being drawn to him. If life weren't as hectic as it was for her, she could see herself being drawn to him *a lot*.

"Still, I'd better think on this wish before making it," she teased.

"Take as long as you like," he told her magnanimously. "There's no expiration date on it."

And if it kept her interacting with him—with them, Steve amended, throwing his son into the mix—until she decided on her wish, well, then it was all to the good, wasn't it?

She nodded her head as if taking it all in. "Good to know."

He smiled at her. Then his tone sobered ever so slightly as he said, "I had a really nice time tonight."

Since he'd said that, she felt it safe to admit, "Me too."

He didn't exactly know why—since in reality he barely knew her—but he felt close to her, closer than he had to a lot of other women he'd known longer and better. "I can't remember the last time I did, actually," he said.

Since they were being so honest, she felt she could admit to that, as well. "Me, too."

He grinned at her a little uncertainly. "Are you just being polite? Or—?"

"Or," she chose. It was getting late and she was still standing here on the curb beside her car. If she didn't get going, she was liable to spend the rest of the evening here, talking about nothing and enjoying it immensely. "Now I'd better go before my car turns into a pumpkin."

"I thought it was a coach that turned into a pumpkin."

"I was upgraded," she answered with almost a straight face. "But the mice must be really worried by now," she said, pressing the release button on her key chain to disarm her car alarm. Four locks rose and stood at attention.

"Can't have worried mice," he agreed. "It interferes with their productivity." And then he laughed. He couldn't remember *when* he'd enjoyed talking such nonsense before. "You certainly are unique."

"Funny, I was just thinking the same thing about you." After she got into her car, she was about to close the door when she saw him stopping it at the last moment. "Something wrong?"

"Other than you leaving too soon? No." Steve caught himself and regrouped. "I'd like to see you again," he told her. "Would that be all right with you?"

All sorts of excuses rose to her lips, excuses about production schedules and meetings and having to do presentations for another toy-store chain. But what ultimately came out was, "That would be very all right with me."

Then, embarrassed by the way she'd blurted that out, Erin pulled the door out of his hand with a quick yank, shutting it. The next second, she was pulling away from the curb.

But she did glance up into the rearview mirror a couple of times to see if Steve was still standing there at the curb.

He was.

Her heart managed to skip a beat each time she did look.

She kept glancing up into the mirror until she could no longer see him.

Chapter Nine

Erin had just fished out the key to her house and was about to put it in the front door lock when she heard the phone inside ringing.

Her adrenaline automatically sped up as she quickly pushed the key into the lock.

She had an answering machine and knew how to retrieve missed messages with the best of them, and more likely than not, the person on the other end of the line was either a wrong number or someone trying to get her to donate to some foundation created to look after retired, one-legged, cross-eyed carrier pigeons.

But whenever she heard her phone ringing, Erin always felt she had to do her very best to pick up the receiver before the person on the other end of the line hung up, no matter what.

Now was no exception.

Hurrying, Erin managed to unlock her door and get to the phone just as the fourth ring was kicking in. At that point, the call was being routed to voice mail.

She grabbed the receiver anyway and rather than waiting out the message, she tried to talk above her own voice, which was leaving instructions that every individual over the age of three knew by heart.

Hearing the shrilled piercing beep go off after her recorded message ended, Erin tried talking to the caller again.

"Hello, are you still there?" When she didn't hear anything, she tried one last time. "Hello?"

This time, she heard someone respond. "Is this too soon?"

Already agitated, her heart stopped in midbeat, then sped up to make up for it. She paused for a moment, thinking she had to be imagining things. Still, she knew she had to ask.

"Steve?"

"Yes, it's me." She could almost *hear* his smile. "Is this too soon?"

She had no idea what he was talking about. "Too soon for what?"

"Too soon to invite you back?"

All but hugging the receiver against her ear, Erin felt warm all over. And she knew if she grinned any wider, she was in danger of rupturing her cheeks. Obviously he'd been serious when he told her that he'd had a nice time.

Still, she downplayed the moment. "You really hate to cook that much, huh?"

"Oh, I wasn't inviting you back to cook for us," he

told her. "Although that certainly is an idea to keep on the back burner. I was actually thinking of inviting you out to a movie."

She hadn't been exaggerating about having an extremely busy schedule. It was a given and had been for the past three years of her life, but suddenly, confronted with this impromptu invitation, for the life of her she couldn't remember a single thing she had written down on that schedule.

The only thing that she *could* remember was that warm feeling she'd had sitting at the dining room table with Steve and his son, talking. Laughing. For just the briefest instant, she knew exactly what it was that her mother kept telling her she was missing out on. She was missing out on the feeling of making a connection, of having a family to talk to, a family to just sit in silence with.

Maybe someday...

"Do you have any particular movie in mind?" she asked him.

"That's strictly up to you," he said. "Anything you want to see is fine with me," Steve assured her.

She didn't even have to think. She knew. "How do you feel about going to see *The Magic Carpet?*"

There was a long pause on the other end, as if he was trying to find just the right words to bring up what could be a delicate subject. "You do know that's a cartoon, right?"

"I know," she told him. "I thought that Jason might enjoy seeing that one better than some of the other movies that are currently playing in the nearby theaters."

"Jason?" Steve asked, puzzled.

"Yes. Jason. Your son," she added for good measure, doing her best to hide her amusement. "Short guy, seven going on eight, nice smile—"

"I know who Jason is," he said with a confused laugh. "But I'm just kind of surprised that you'd want to take him along with us to the movies."

They'd gotten along very well at Steve's house. She didn't understand why he didn't just automatically include the boy in this invitation he was extending.

"Why does that surprise you?" she asked him.

"Most women would look at bringing a seven-year-old along as a veiled attempt at babysitting," Steve told her frankly.

"I'm not most women," Erin pointed out.

Which was why he was breaking his own promise to himself about taking a break from this whole soul-wearying concept of dating and asking this woman out. Because she was so very different from the rest.

"No, you are not," he agreed heartily. Still, he wanted to make sure this wasn't something she felt as if she *had* to do. "Are you sure you want to see *The Magic Carpet?*"

"Oh, I'm sure, all right," she said, then added whimsically, "Don't forget, I'm the one who spends her time talking to stuffed dinosaurs."

"I'm definitely not about to forget that part," he told her. Because as far as he was concerned, he and Jason were damn lucky that she did. At least for now, it appeared that the video game with its threatening aliens had fallen by the wayside. "I'll let you pick the date and time," he told her.

She didn't have to think about that, either. "Well, it would have to be on the weekend," she reminded him, "since we both work and I'm sure that your job is probably even more demanding than mine," she said, not wanting to sound as if she were giving herself airs as to her own importance, "so making plans to catch an evening show would be difficult, not to mention that it would most likely be past Jason's bedtime."

She'd managed to impress him again. Granted, what she'd just said took only a very simple calculation but it was also something that most single women wouldn't even think of.

Hell, most single women wouldn't be willing to sit through ninety-seven minutes' worth of death-defying antics by a wise-cracking hero who happened to be in possession of a magic flying carpet that flew to his rescue every time.

"Saturday, then?" he assumed.

"Sunday would be better, if that's all right with you," she prefaced, then explained, "Sometimes we have to have emergency Saturday meetings."

She'd managed to pique his curiosity again. "Out of sheer curiosity, what constitutes an emergency in the world of stuffed-dinosaur manufacturing?"

She supposed that had come across a bit melodramatic. "Well, for one thing, we're starting to fall behind in meeting our orders."

"That many people want your product?" he asked in surprise.

"Yes, isn't it wonderful?" she cried with enthusiasm. "I never thought I'd feel like I couldn't keep up production to meet the demand, but that day is starting to draw closer and closer—thank God."

"Then I guess you need to hire more people, you know, expand," Steve suggested. From where he stood, that seemed like a simple enough solution.

"We've thought about that," she answered, "but to be honest, I'm afraid that if we go ahead and hire a couple more workers, it just might jinx us and suddenly, people will stop buying Tex and his friends and we'll be stuck with a whole bunch of dinosaurs that nobody wants to buy anymore."

He gleaned a piece of insight out of her answer. "You're superstitious?" Steve asked.

"Just a tiny bit," she admitted. "I mean, I have no problem with walking under ladders or stopping to pet black cats or ignoring spilled salt on a table—other than just to clean it up. But taking too much for granted and expanding the company kind of feels as if I'm just thumbing my nose at fate or whatever is behind all this success we've been having. It just seems to be too cocky for me to think this sort of demand can continue indefinitely."

"Cocky?" he repeated with a laugh. "You? Somehow *cocky* isn't the first word that comes to mind in describing you—or the tenth word, for that matter. I think it's just common sense, not cocky. Think about it," he advised. "Hiring more people might be something that you and your company need to look into in order to meet your commitments and deadlines. You really don't want to get on the wrong end of that. Not being able to meet your commitments might hurt your reputation and at this point in the game, your reputation is everything."

"How much do I owe you for that legal advice, counselor?" she teased.

"Consider it on the house," he told her. Then, in case her sense of honor made her object to that, he reminded her, "After all, you didn't let me pay for the dinosaur."

"As long as Jason gives Tex Jr. a good home, we'll call it even."

"No worries there," Steve assured her. "He's already asked me if I'd buy Tex his own bed tomorrow."

"I hope you told him that he has to double up for a while," she said.

"I did and he seemed okay with that." Even as he related the story, it still left him somewhat in awe. He had his old Jason back and the relief he felt was unbelievable. It wasn't anything he *ever* planned to take for granted. "Really, Erin, I can't thank you enough for bringing that toy into my son's life. He's like the little boy I knew again."

That was more than reward enough for her. "Glad I could help."

Even though he appreciated the gesture, Steve felt he should ask one more time—just to be certain. "And you're sure about wanting to see that kid movie?"

"Absolutely," she said with feeling. "I'm looking forward to seeing it and looking forward to seeing Jason—and you, too," she added in case he had any doubts.

She wanted to go very slowly here, not just because there was a child involved but because the thought of dating left her more than a wee bit nervous. Having the boy along helped ease her tension. She was better with kids than she was with adults—unless she'd known them for years, the way she had the people she worked with.

"I've got the listing for Sunday right here," he was telling her. "You want to pick a time so you can pencil it into your schedule?"

"I'm not planning on penciling it in," Erin said to him.

Had she changed her mind already? he wondered. "Oh?"

"No. Pencil can be erased. I'll be using my permanent marker for this," she said, just in case he didn't think she was being serious about looking forward to the outing.

Steve started reading off the showtimes. "First showing's at ten-thirty. Is that too early for you?" he asked.

"You consider ten-thirty early?" she said incredulously. "By ten-thirty I usually have about five to six hours of work done."

"On a Sunday?" he questioned, impressed by her dedication.

"*Especially* on a Sunday," she emphasized, then explained, "No major interruptions."

"I'll have to remember that," he said with a touch of amusement. "I'll call you on Saturday night to confirm."

Although she liked hearing the sound of his voice, there was no need for him to call, if he thought she was going to reconsider.

"Consider it already confirmed. I'm not about to pass up seeing a feel-good movie with two handsome men," she told him.

"I'll be sure to pass that along to Jason. If *he* starts to act cocky, that's on you," Steve told her. And then he went on to ask, "Out of curiosity, since you actually seem to *want* to see this movie, why haven't you gone to see it already? It's been out in the theaters a couple of weeks already."

"I don't mind shopping alone. I've gotten used to doing things like that. But there is something exceptionally lonely about going to the movies all by myself," she said. "I just can't bring myself to do it. Besides, a movie is too much of an indulgence, considering the kind of work schedule I have."

"Okay, I'll still call you on Saturday night, but it'll be just to talk."

If he was calling her on Saturday night just to talk, that meant that there really wasn't anyone else around for him to spend time with. Erin caught herself smiling broadly.

"I'll talk to you then," she told him.

After hanging up the phone, she stood there for a moment just smiling at it.

Erin was grateful that there was no one around right now to observe her because she probably looked like some sort of an idiot, smiling like that at an inanimate object.

"Oh, like talking to stuffed dinosaurs is any more normal," she mocked herself, using Tex's voice to put her in her place.

But Tex—the *idea* of Tex, she silently insisted—

had paved the way to what was on its way, for all intents, to become a very lucrative business someday. If anything, what she'd told Steve was downplaying the truth. Orders were coming in so fast and furious, Judith, Neal and Christian were barely keeping up the production end.

And what she'd told Steve *was* the truth. She really *was* afraid to hire more people, afraid that once she took those people on, for some unknown reason business would begin to fall off and then she would be forced to let those people she'd just hired go.

She wasn't any good at firing people.

Actually, she doubted if there was anyone worse at it than she was. She'd done it only once before and it had been agony for her, even though Wade Baker more than deserved to be fired for so many reasons. It wasn't just because he wasn't a team player and kept telling everyone else what to do. His greatest offense was that he wanted to get familiar in ways that had nothing to do with the company and everything to do with her.

She'd fired him and he'd refused to leave. It had gotten to the point that she had to threaten him with a restraining order because he'd kept showing up at work and then even her home.

Each time, he grew more and more belligerent and nasty until it got to a very unbearable point.

But her life had been Wade-free for a couple of months now and she truly hoped it would remain that way for many years to come.

Maybe he'd found a new cause to espouse and a

new person to annoy. Why he was gone didn't matter. The only thing that mattered was that he was gone.

With a yawn, she went to the kitchen to prepare her usual cup of tea before bedtime. It was her way of unwinding, and tonight she felt like a giant metal coil that had to unwind for more than a couple of minutes. This just might turn into a major undertaking.

Once the tea was brewed, she poured it into a cup that had Dorothy's famous words about not being in Kansas anymore written on the side.

As Erin took her first sip of chai tea, a thought struck her. Her mouth curved even as she lowered the large cup.

She had a date.

A real live date. Her mother was going to be thrilled.

But as she reached for the phone to call her mother, a little voice inside her head warned, *No! Don't do it. Not yet.*

Erin paused, debating. The little voice was probably right. As much as she loved sharing things with her mother and as happy as she knew her mother would be over this news after spending the past several years lamenting about her single status and the fact that she wasn't doing anything at all to even attempt to change that status, Erin also knew that her mother had the ability to get utterly carried away with the least amount of provocation. And in her mother's eyes, this would be more than just a little.

If she said *anything* at all about going out on a date, she felt certain that her mother would be out there like a shot, searching nonstop for the perfect wedding dress as well as interviewing different pastry chefs in an attempt to zero in on what would be the perfect wedding cake.

Erin blew out a long breath, making up her mind. It was far better to let her mother know about this *after* the fact rather than before.

Because the phone had been ringing when she first walked in, Erin realized that she'd completely forgotten about picking up her mail.

Not that it mattered all that much. There were probably just bills and miscellaneous catalogs she had no interest in stuffed into her mailbox.

It certainly wasn't anything that wouldn't keep until the morning.

Still, because the mailbox was small, she knew that if she *didn't* empty it now and left tomorrow without getting the mail—something she was more than likely to do because she had done it once or twice before— there wouldn't be much room for the mail carrier to leave whatever mail would arrive that day.

She didn't like creating problems.

So with a sigh, Erin got her mail key out. Reluctantly, she stepped back into her shoes, then walked out of her house and made her way down the driveway to her mailbox.

The moment the sun had gone down, it had grown chilly outside, a subtle hint from Mother Nature that summer wasn't meant to hang around indefinitely and that cooler days were just around the corner.

Opening her front door, she heard what sounded like the howl of a coyote off in the distance. She'd spotted one or two in the area since she'd moved here.

For the most part, she knew they lived somewhere around the greenbelt but except for those two sightings, she had been coyote-free.

Hearing one howl now sent a chill down her spine. Was that some sort of an omen?

You're not superstitious, remember?

Erin darted to the curb and her mailbox.

She opened the slender rectangular door, grabbed the handful of envelopes she found there, pushed the door back into place and hurried back to the house. She tossed the mail as well as the key on the coffee table, thinking she'd look at it in the morning.

But something caught her eye.

It was an envelope, off-white in color, whose shape—square and small—stood out. It didn't resemble the rest of the envelopes. The others came from companies—those providing a service and others looking to make a connection. This one came from an individual.

For one thing, it was handwritten.

There was no return address.

Curious, Erin debated just leaving it where it was, but in the end, she opened it.

The next moment, she really wished that she hadn't.

There was only one line written in the middle of the page. The sender had used all capital block letters.

YOU SHOULD HAVE BEEN NICE TO ME WHEN YOU HAD THE CHANCE.

Chapter Ten

There was nothing else tucked inside the envelope or written on the outside of it. Neither was there anything written on the single sheet of paper besides the one ominous sentence, all in capitals.

Erin blew out a breath, doing her best not to panic. "Okay, not a fan letter," she said, refolding the paper and slipping it carefully back into the envelope. She made sure to hold on to only a corner of the letter so as not to get any more of her fingerprints on it than she already had.

It was probably nothing, she silently insisted. But if her life were being lived out in an episodic police procedural, this letter might be the only clue that would help the investigative detectives track down her killer—after the fact.

"Way to go to make yourself crazy, Erin. This is

probably just Wade's stupid idea of making me feel paranoid and nervous," she said out loud. For once she hadn't fallen back on using Tex's voice.

Even so, she put the envelope away in the top drawer of her bureau in plain sight—just in case.

Closing the drawer, she blew out another long, steadying breath. She was *not* going to think about what was in the note and allow it to ruin what had turned out to be one of the best *personal* days she'd had in a long time.

She couldn't help herself.

Try as she might not to let it, the contents of the envelope—and the intent behind it—preyed on her mind for most of the night.

The darker the night grew, the darker the thoughts that assailed her became.

What if it wasn't Wade? What if the note was sent by some random crazy person? Stranger things had happened. There were people out there whose twisted thinking processes were way beyond her comprehension. She belonged in a world where people responded to grinning dinosaurs wearing cowboy hats, to kindness rather than cruelty.

But since the envelope *was* actually addressed to her, the possibility that it was all a big mistake seemed slim and she also rather doubted that this had been done by a complete stranger. These days strangers were far more likely to hack into a computer, planting some sort of a virus or unleashing a scam, than rely on something evolving via snail mail.

So who would be threatening her like this?

She couldn't get herself to believe that it was actually Wade, yet right now, that seemed to be the only logical answer.

"Not going to think about it," Erin told the bleary-eyed reflection that stared back at her in her bathroom mirror the following morning. "Yeah, right," she murmured as she put away her toothbrush and forced herself to get ready for work.

Work was her saving grace. Work was what she turned to whenever anything else was bothering her. Because when she was working, she forgot about everything else except for the joy that the toys she was creating would bring.

She hardly remembered locking her front door and getting into her car, let alone making the trip to the ground-floor office Imagine That occupied.

"Wow, you look like hell, Fearless Leader. Did you get *any* sleep last night?" Mike asked her when she walked into the office.

Accustomed to coming into an empty office, Erin swallowed a gasp of surprise when she suddenly realized that she wasn't alone.

Getting hold of her bearings, she took a long look at Mike. He looked rumpled—and then it dawned on her that it was his shirt that was rumpled, as if it had been slept in.

"You should talk," she countered. "At least I went home. Isn't that the same shirt you were wearing yesterday?"

"Maybe I have more than one shirt this same color," he answered defensively.

That was a nonanswer—which meant only one thing. "Not answering my question *is* answering my question," she told Mike.

Mike shook his head, turning his attention back to what he'd been doing when she walked in. "Gotta get you to stop watching those cop shows," he muttered. Since she was obviously waiting for some sort of an explanation, he gave her the bare bones of one. "I was trying to work out something and maybe time got away from me. I suppose I kind of fell asleep at my desk," he admitted.

Having crossed to his desk, she got a better look at him. "That would explain the paper-clip imprint on your cheek," she decided, then asked, "Exactly *what* is it that you were trying to work out?"

"He didn't want to tell you," Rhonda's voice said directly behind her.

Erin turned to find the woman standing in the doorway, taking everything in. This was quite early for Rhonda, too, she couldn't help thinking. What the hell was going on?

"Tell me what?" she asked the other woman. Her tone left no room for evasiveness.

So Rhonda told her the truth. "Someone is suing us. The company," she emphasized.

"Suing us?" Erin echoed, stunned and utterly bewildered. "Suing us for what?" she asked. "For making overly cute stuffed dinosaurs? There's absolutely nothing even remotely hazardous about Tex and his friends," she declared, her mind instantly jumping to the conclusion that the suit involved some consumer agency. "Other than perhaps their being terminally adorable. Last time I checked, that wasn't a reason for either recall or shutting down the factory."

By now Christian, looking as world-weary as the rest of them, had joined the group and fielded the question. "We're not being sued by a parent or some EPA-type group," he told Erin.

"Then what's going on?" she asked. "Just who is suing us?"

She got no further with her questions. Looking as if he was bracing himself, Christian gave her an answer. One she wouldn't have begun to guess and found repugnant once she knew it.

"Wade Baker is behind the suit," he said.

Erin was aware of her mouth dropping open. Closing it, she stared at Christian. That just didn't make *any* sense whatsoever.

"You're kidding." But even as she said it, she had a sinking feeling that it was true. Still, she crossed her fingers mentally.

It didn't help.

"Wish I were," Christian told her with sincerity.

"What could Wade possibly be suing about? That I fired him because he was not only lazy and disrespectful to the rest of you but because his idea of hands-on experience meant having his hands on me?" she cried. "If anything, we should be suing *him,* not the other way around."

Christian shook his head. He sat down next to Mike and Rhonda. "Apparently, according to the suit, Baker claims that Tex the T. rex was actually originally *his* idea."

"His idea?" she repeated incredulously. The man

hadn't had a single original idea the entire time he'd worked for her. "If Wade had an idea of any kind, it would have died of loneliness in his head," she said angrily.

It was obvious that Mike was wrestling with something and just as obvious that he came to the conclusion that she might as well know the worst of it sooner rather than later.

He avoided her eyes as he told her, "Well, it seems that Baker claims that you stole it from him after the two of you…made love," he mumbled after hesitating a moment. "He said he told you his idea while the two of you were having pillow talk."

Utterly speechless, Erin couldn't even find the words to describe her disgust for several seconds. Finally she managed to croak out a stunned "What?"

"You want me to repeat it?" Mike asked her uncertainly.

"No, I want you to shoot him." Numbed, Erin shook her head. This was insane. "Unless that man owns a talking pillow, there was never any so-called pillow talk between us. There was never even a *pillow* between us." She shivered as she tried to rid herself of the very *thought* of what the suit suggested.

"Hey, you don't have to prove anything to us," Christian assured her.

"We *know* you have better taste than that," Rhonda said, adding her voice to the chorus.

Erin sighed, still shaken—and swiftly working her way to livid. "I'm not trying to prove anything. I'm stating it flatly. Wade is just doing this because I fired him after he tried to get more up close and personal with me than I ever wanted to. It's his way of getting even."

But even as she uttered the words, the underlying result of all this deeply concerned her. The reason this was happening didn't change things. Baker could still ruin her and cause everyone who worked with her to lose their jobs, all because the man's ego had been hurt.

She looked at the three people in the room with her and thought of the three others who were out of sight for the moment. They *depended* on her, believed in her in the lean times, had gone without pay at times so the company could get off the ground. She just *couldn't* allow that egotistical maniac to win.

"When did you find out about this?" she asked Mike, since he'd obviously been the first one to know.

"Yesterday, after you left the office," Mike told her. He looked at the others before continuing. "Baker's lawyer showed up to serve us with papers. According to him, we're supposed to shut down the company until this is settled."

Her eyes widened with anger. That was *not* about to happen. "We can't shut down production," Erin cried. "We've got a ton of orders to fill."

"I know that," Mike said, producing the papers that Wade's lawyer had left with him. He got up from behind his desk, crossed to Erin and gave them to her. "But I've got to admit, this looks pretty intimidating, as did his lawyer."

Erin skimmed the first page. The words all swam in front of her eyes. Nothing was going to make sense right now. She was too upset for the words to sink in and register.

"The guy's probably just some ambulance chaser," she commented dismissively.

"If he is, then he's capable of catching those ambulances with his bare hands," Christian told her. "The guy looked like some kind of hulking giant. About six-four and close to three hundred pounds. Not somebody you want to mess with."

Erin was growing progressively angrier. This lawyer, whoever he was, was threatening something she held dear, not to mention intimidating people she cared about by threatening their livelihood.

She looked at Mike. "You should have called me," she told him.

"We hoped that maybe we could get this to go away. You've got enough to think about," Mike said, "trying to get those chain toy stores to partner up with us."

"Do the others know?" she asked, referring to Judith, Neal and Gypsy.

Mike nodded. "Everybody but you."

"Erin, do we have enough money set aside in the kitty to hire a top-notch lawyer to fight this?" Rhonda asked.

"Forget top-notch—do we have enough money to hire *any* lawyer to fight this?" Christian asked.

Other than taking out enough to cover their salaries and pay for her mortgage as well as buy food, she had been plowing all their profits back into the company with an eye out to expand Imagine That enough to impress Toyland Toys, the other toy-store chain she'd set her sights on.

Erin's eyes swept over the three people in the room. She'd started this company with a dream and three friends who were willing to help her make that dream flourish. It couldn't end like this.

And yet...

It killed her to admit this, but she wasn't about to start lying to people she cared about. "Right now we have enough money to buy a round of lattes for all of us—as long as we're satisfied with the medium size."

"Great," Christian mumbled, sinking farther down on his chair.

"What are we going to do?" Rhonda asked.

Christian raised his hand as if they were back in elementary school. When she looked at him, he said, "I've got this cousin who knows this guy who could send Baker off on a one-way cruise as long as we pay for the steamer trunk."

Erin frowned. That was a nonstarter. "Much as I'd like to, we're not sticking him into a trunk. That would only make things worse," she told Christian.

"Then what are we going to do?" Christian challenged.

Erin blew out a frustrated breath. What she would have liked to do was pummel Wade into the ground. "I could try reasoning with Wade."

"That's presupposing that the jerk has reason," Mike pointed out. "Remember, this is the guy who doesn't work well or play well with others." His dark brown eyes met hers. "The guy I would have kicked to the curb on day one if you hadn't been as softhearted as you were," Mike reminded her.

Erin was keenly aware that at bottom, this was her fault. She was not the type to buck pass. "I know and I'm sorry. I just thought all he needed was a little time," she told Mike.

"Twenty to life comes to mind," Rhonda quipped.

"You sure you don't want me to call my cousin?" Christian asked her hopefully.

It was a tempting idea but not the kind, ultimately, she could live with. "I'm sure." Desperate, she cast about for a solution—

And then she thought of Steve. The man was a lawyer. At the very least, maybe he would have a suggestion on how she could extricate herself and her company from what was beginning to sound as if it could turn into an abysmal legal mess and call a halt to production—something she had a feeling was ultimately Wade's goal in all this. He wanted to hurt her where she "lived."

"I'm going to make a call," she announced.

"*You* know a hit man?" Mike asked with renewed hope in his voice.

"No," she said patiently, "I know a lawyer."

"Hit men are more reliable," Mike said.

"As much as I do relish the idea of strangling Wade with my bare hands," she admitted, "I don't think they'll let us manufacture Tex and his friends from prison."

"Hey, who's to say? After all, they make license plates in prison, don't they?" Rhonda pointed out.

Erin looked at the trio. God, but she loved these

people. There was no way she was going to see all their efforts get swept away like sand castles before a tidal wave.

"You know," she told them, "as a cheering section, you guys really leave something to be desired."

Mike was hardly listening as he shook his head. "I knew I should have beaten Baker to a pulp when I found out what he was trying to get you to do."

She patted the man's face. "Not that I don't appreciate the thought, Mike, but we also don't have money to bail you out of jail, and Baker was the type to play dirty."

"I think my grandmother has an old steamer trunk in her storage unit," Christian called after her as Erin walked away to her office.

Instead of responding to the offer, Erin raised her hand above her head and waved at him. Or, more precisely, waved away the thought.

In the tiny glass-walled enclosure that served as her so-called private office, Erin sat down and pulled out the card that Steve had given her. She looked at it for a long moment. This was probably going to kill the movie date, she thought, but she'd already made up her mind. They needed the company more than she needed to go out on a date with him.

With anyone, she amended, striving to put distance between herself and what she was about to do.

Taking a deep breath, she hit the numbers on the keypad of her landline.

She assumed that she would be connecting to the law firm's secretary and prepared herself for a female's voice. Instead what she heard was Steve's deep voice on the other end of the line. The second she did, Erin felt her pulse start accelerating.

The reaction was automatic.

She needed to get control over that, Erin told herself.

"Hi," she said, her mouth growing even drier than it already was. "Is this a bad time?"

Now, there was a conversation stopper, she upbraided herself. He was going to think he was talking to a mental midget.

There was a slight pause and then she heard Steve ask, "Erin? Is that you?"

Considering that they had only talked on the phone once, that was a remarkable guess on his part. "You're very good," she told him.

He thought it wiser not to tell her that she'd been on his mind since last night, not just because his son kept talking about her last night as well as this morning, but because even if Jason hadn't said a single word in reference to her, she still would have been lingering on his mind like a deep perfume that had infiltrated all his senses.

It was still early in the game and saying something like that might very well spook her. Not to mention that he might, after all, be reacting prematurely, giving her more credit than she deserved.

But with his other less-than-thrilling experiences in the dating world, it was easy to see why he would get carried away with Erin. She was bright and witty, and she had made a connection with his son.

"I've got a good memory for voices," he told her,

shrugging off her compliment. "So what can I do for you?" he asked.

"I need some advice."

"Go ahead—I'm listening," he urged.

"Turns out I'm being sued."

"As of this morning?" Steve asked, a sliver of skepticism entering his mind. She hadn't mentioned anything about being sued last night. It seemed like the perfect opportunity, if what she was saying now was the truth.

Or had last night been all about setting him up just for this? Had she just been pretending with his son in order to get on his good side? He disliked being this suspicious, but he disliked getting burned even more. Besides, this wasn't about just him. It was *never* about just him anymore. He had to think in the plural because everything he did affected Jason.

"Actually," she answered, "as strange as it sounds, yes. I didn't find out about this until just this morning."

Okay, he'd play along for now. Who knew? Maybe she *was* telling the truth. "Who's suing you?"

"It's a little complicated to get into over the phone," she told him. "By any chance, are you free for lunch?"

As he spoke, he took out his cell phone and glanced at the entries on his daily calendar. He had something scheduled for noon, but it wasn't written in stone and could easily be rescheduled.

"I could be," he allowed, then remembered what she had told him yesterday about her time constraints. "I thought you said that you were really busy," he reminded her.

Erin laughed shortly. "If this suit goes through and he wins, then the only thing I'll be busy doing is looking for a job."

Erin's fear was almost palpable. He was beginning to believe her. She was either very good or very worried. "That bad?" he asked.

She thought of putting up a brave front, but he was, for all intents, almost a stranger and she had to be able to let her hair down with someone. He, at least, wasn't going to be affected by anything that happened, one way or the other. She didn't have to be the brave trooper, soldiering on for him.

"Worse than bad," she confessed.

"Hold on a second—let me see what I can do with my schedule," he said.

"I don't want to disrupt anything," she protested belatedly. When she received no answer, she realized that she was talking to dead air. He'd put her on hold.

This was a bad idea, she told herself. She was imposing on a man she hardly knew—and most likely wouldn't get to know since he probably thought, at the very least, that she was using him.

The problem was that she didn't know anyone else to turn to. She supposed that maybe her mother knew—

"I'm back," Steve declared. "I've cleared ten o'clock to eleven o'clock this morning. Can you get down here by ten?"

Even if she couldn't, she would. After all, he'd put himself out for her.

"Absolutely," she told him.

"Okay, then, I'll see you at ten," he said. He had

to admit, at this point his curiosity was more than just a little piqued.

"I really appreciate you making time for me like this."

"I was at the end of my rope with Jason. You managed to bring him back around and on top of that, you made it seem effortless on your part," he said quite honestly. "Trying to help you out is the very least I can do."

"No, it really means a lot," she countered. "It's not as if I have any legal counsel to turn to. Thank you," she told him, feeling that the paltry words weren't nearly enough. But she had no others at her disposal. With the threat of an embarrassing spate of dead air stretching out between them, she quickly hung up.

Though he wasn't happy about it, both his life and his vocation had taught him to be suspicious, which in turn had him wondering again about this phone call from Erin. Hopefully, he thought, returning the receiver back into the cradle, he wasn't going to regret this.

He still hadn't quite made up his mind about that yet.

Chapter Eleven

A little more than an hour later, Erin was walking into the ground floor of Steve's building, a recently constructed office tower that was the last word in savvy architectural design. The outer walls were all dark, smoky glass. It looked as if it should have been home to an art museum instead of various professionals.

More than one law firm was listed in the first-floor directory. The one Steve was associated with had the largest letters, she noted.

I can't afford this, Erin thought, getting on the elevator.

She was even more convinced that she couldn't afford Steve's services when she got off the elevator. It appeared that Steve's law firm rented the entire fourth floor.

Erin approached the long, regal-looking reception desk that was facing the elevator bank on slightly shaky legs. Behind the desk were twelve-inch-high frosted silver letters that proclaimed the name of the firm: Donnal, Wiseman, Monroe and Finnegan, the four senior partners who had initially started the firm.

She probably didn't have enough money in Imagine That's assets to pay for the sign, much less the services of one of the lawyers associated with the sign.

This was a mistake, Erin thought. She shouldn't have come.

For one fleeting moment, she thought of turning around and heading back down in the elevator, but her getaway was curtailed because at that exact moment, the sleek redhead behind the desk looked up from her keyboard and saw her.

"May I help you?" She asked the question in a slow, deliberate cadence.

Well, she was here—she might as well go through with the rest of it, Erin told herself. "I'm here to see Steven Kendall."

The woman, an administrative assistant by the name of Ruby Royce, regarded her dispassionately for a second, as if taking measure of her. "Do you have an appointment?" she finally asked her in a calm, cool voice.

Erin pressed her lips together. "I'm not sure you could call it an appointment exactly." Damn it, she was tripping over her own tongue, something she did when facing another adult without the benefit of a stuffed dinosaur in her hands. Taking a breath, she tried again. "I mean—"

"She has an appointment, Ruby," Steve said, walking up behind the receptionist. "She's my ten o'clock," he specified.

"Hi," Erin said with visible relief when she saw Steve coming to her rescue.

"Funny, she doesn't look like a Harvey Rothstein," Ruby observed wryly.

As far as administrative assistants went, there was none better than Ruby. All the associates made use of her skills. With that in mind, he played along with her wry observation.

"Mr. Rothstein was good enough to let me move his appointment to twelve o'clock," he told Ruby. "You might want to make a notation of that on your schedule."

Ruby nodded, doing just that. "I wish you'd let me know before you decide to play musical chairs with your appointments, Mr. Kendall."

"I'm letting you know now, Ruby," he told her, unfazed. "I'll try to improve my timing the next time around." Looking at Erin, he said, "All right, let's go into my office and you can tell me all about what has you so upset."

Erin nodded, falling into step beside him as he led the way from the reception area down the hall to his office. But as they walked away from the reception area, she could swear she felt Ruby's eyes watching her every move.

"I don't think she likes me," Erin told him in a low, hushed voice.

"It's nothing personal," he assured her as they turned down the hall. "Ruby just doesn't like being caught off guard, that's all. It interferes with her self-image—that of being the world's best administrative assistant. Just between you and me, for the most part, she really is.

"Right this way," he said, gesturing toward the office on his right.

Erin had almost walked right by it. She backtracked a couple of steps and crossed the threshold into the spacious, airy yet decidedly masculine office.

Feeling just a little intimidated, Erin paused inside the doorway, looking around.

"Something wrong?" he asked her, curious.

"No," she answered a little too quickly, then said, "I was just thinking that my whole company could probably fit into this office with room to spare."

Steve gestured toward the chair on the other side of his desk as he sank into the soft leather of his recently purchased chair. "The firm's been around for close to fifty years. They've had time to build up."

Erin began to follow suit and sit down. But, her hands still gripping the armrests, she stopped in mid-motion, perched just *above* the actual seat. She reverted back to her feeling that coming here was most likely a mistake.

She might as well give him the negative news first. "I can't afford to pay you," Erin told him. "I mean, not right away. Not all of it," she corrected herself again. God, but she wished she could have words deftly slide from her tongue rather than come out in choppy bits and pieces when she was nervous.

"What I'm trying to say is that I don't have much available cash. Almost all the money I make gets plowed right back into the company, but I can pay you in installments—probably a lot of them," she guessed, looking around at the sleek bookcase and the volumes of leather-bound law books that were neatly arranged on the shelves. "No matter how long it takes, I *will* pay your bill off," she promised earnestly, "but if you decided that's not how you do things, I'll understand," Erin concluded. She wanted him to understand that she wasn't looking for special treatment.

"Are you finished?" he asked when she finally paused for air.

"Out of breath," she admitted.

Steve nodded. "Same thing," he allowed. "For now, why don't you tell me the problem that has you so worried? We'll talk about terms and fees later."

"Okay." She didn't let go of the armrests, even as she sank down in the chair. "I'm being sued." The words felt as if they were sticking to the roof of her mouth, scraping the skin there.

"By who?" he asked.

"By Wade Baker." Even his name left a bitter taste in her mouth.

"Is that someone you know?" he asked, trying to get a few more details out of Erin.

"Yes." She took a deep breath, then added, "I fired him."

His eyes never leaving hers, Steve rocked back slightly in his chair. "I see."

"I didn't want to," she told him, her voice gaining back some of its momentum. "I really hated firing Wade, but he gave me no choice."

Waiting for her to continue, he coaxed, "I'm listening."

Did he want background? She could give him that, Erin thought. "Wade was one of the first people I hired. We all go way back."

"'All'?" Steve questioned.

"The rest of the people at Imagine That and I." That sounded awkward to her, so she elaborated a little more. "We all went to college together. When I started the company, I turned to them and we went into business together," she explained.

"And then you fired Wade," he supplied.

That made it sound abrupt and whimsical—it was anything *but* that. "Well, not right away. We worked together for three years, long nights, living on mustard sandwiches, things like that," she said. "It was pretty tough going and, to be honest, I thought about quitting a couple of times. I think most of us did," she admitted.

"And then about a year ago, after a reporter ran a story about Tex that got picked up by a national TV newscast, we were finally on our way. Sales jumped, then doubled more than a couple of times. We were having trouble keeping up with the orders." And it felt like heaven, she couldn't help thinking.

"Tell me about the suit," Steve urged. "Why is this Wade Baker person suing you?" he asked.

It upset her to even talk about it, but ignoring it wasn't going to make the problem go away. "Wade claims that Tex and a couple of the other toys were really his idea."

"But they weren't." It wasn't an assumption or a

question. He was just stating what he assumed she was going to maintain.

"No!" Erin cried. "They weren't. Like I told you the other day, I came up with Tex when I was ten, maybe closer to eleven years old. I was in the hospital. My mom came to see me every day, but I just wanted a friend, a friend who wasn't sick, who wasn't getting treatments but who was there for me all the time. I always liked dinosaurs, so one day I made him out of an old green sports sock. Then my mother got some green felt.

"While I was getting my treatments, she would sit in my room waiting for me to come back, working on Tex and keeping him a surprise. When she was done, I added my own touches. Between my mom and me, we gave 'birth' to Tex."

That sounded plausible enough to him. Which left him with another question. "Why do you think Wade's suing you?"

Rather than answer him, Erin took out a sealed plastic baggie from her purse and placed it on his desk. Inside was the letter she'd gotten yesterday.

"What's that?"

"That's a letter I found in my mailbox yesterday. There's no return address and there's only one line written on the page, but I have a feeling that it's from Wade."

Steve took possession of the plastic baggie and pulled out a handkerchief before extracting the envelope and then the single sheet inside the envelope.

He skimmed the note, then looked up at Erin. "My first guess is that you're probably right." He set the note and envelope aside for the time being. "I have to ask this," he prefaced, then continued. "Were you and Wade in a relationship?"

"Not the kind that you mean or that he wanted," Erin told him.

"Could you be a little clearer?"

Not without being nauseated, but then, her comfort wasn't what was at stake here. "Wade thought that because we spent so much time together every day, putting in long hours at the office, that meant I was willing to sleep with him. I wasn't," she said fiercely. She wanted Steve to know that, to know she wasn't the type to take that sort of thing casually. "I regarded him as a friend, not anything more. I thought he'd back off when I didn't respond to his advances and suggestions, but that just made him try harder."

She frowned. "When that didn't work, he got nasty. He'd start getting into arguments with the other people working with us and it got to be so uncomfortable I finally had to let him go. That just made him angrier." She had really felt helpless at that time. "He knows the company means everything to me. Suing me and tying up production is his way of getting back at me. He's going to force me to close the company. Right now I can't meet my orders, can't pay the people working with me. This lawsuit is going to make working a living hell," she lamented.

He'd been nodding thoughtfully at her statements as Erin had quickly filled him in. Now that she'd finished, he offered her a sympathetic smile.

"Let me look into this and see what I can do." He glanced at the letter she'd brought. He'd tucked it back into the baggie, together with the envelope. "Mind if I keep this for now?" he asked, nodding at the baggie. "The firm keeps a couple of top-notch private investigators on retainer and I can get one of them to have a friend of his run the prints, see if we come up with anything."

That all sounded wonderful, but she hesitated giving him the go-ahead. "We haven't discussed your fee yet," she reminded him, afraid that once they did, this feeling that maybe things could be worked out after all would completely vanish.

His fee might be completely out of her league. But she had never been the type to stick her head in the sand and she couldn't just pretend that the practical aspect of all this would just fade away because she wanted it to. If she couldn't afford Steve—and she strongly suspected that she couldn't—she needed to know right now.

"No, we haven't," Steve acknowledged.

Since he wasn't saying anything further on the subject, she asked him, "Shouldn't we?"

"Why don't we just set that aside for the moment?" he suggested.

Erin's back grew instantly straighter, stiffer, as she said, "I know we're pretty much a start-up company and there are no assets per se, but that doesn't mean that I'm looking to accept charity—"

"No one's offering you charity," he quickly told her. *At least, not exactly,* he added silently. "Tell you what. Let me bring this matter up before the firm and I'll get back to you on their decision. In the meantime," he urged her, "try not to worry too much. I've got a good feeling about this."

Optimistic lines like that had ordinarily been her domain. But with her trust trampled on and her faith in people blown to bits, she was finding that remaining optimistic was not nearly as easy to do as it used to be a few short months ago.

"That makes one of us," she murmured in response to his impromptu pep talk.

"Go back to work," he told her. "Rally your troops and I'll get back to you as soon as I have any information to pass on."

She wasn't nearly as naive as she might appear to be at first. "Is that lawyer-speak for 'Don't hold your breath'?" she asked him, actually afraid to allow herself to get hopeful.

"No, that's lawyer-speak for 'I'll get back to you as soon as I have any information to pass on,'" he said patiently. Getting up from his chair, he told her, "I'll walk you out."

But Erin shook her head. "That's okay. I've taken up enough of your time. I can find my way out—I had Tex drop bread crumbs," she said. Then, in a much higher voice, she had Tex say, "And I did—except for the bread crumbs I ate. Hey, I was hungry."

Steve laughed, delighted. "I guess I should consider myself lucky that Tex didn't take a bite out of me while he was at it." Then, sobering just a touch, he asked her, "Are we still on for Sunday and the movie?"

It wasn't that she'd forgotten about the movie date;

it was just that first the note and then the news about getting sued had chased the other thoughts right out of her head.

"Am I allowed to see you after hours?" she asked him.

"I think Jason would insist on it," Steve told her. "As long as he's included."

"Oh, he's definitely included," she assured Steve. Even so, she had to ask, just to be perfectly clear, "So there's no conflict of interest?"

"Not unless you decide you want me to represent this Wade character, too."

"Not a chance," she cried.

"Then we're okay," he said with a wink. "And like I said, try not to worry."

"Easier said than done," she answered, then explained part of the reason she was so anxious. "Wade doesn't like taking no for an answer."

"Neither do I," Steve responded. "But this Wade character is going to have to learn how to do that. By the way, I will get back to you as soon as I know what's going on," he promised. "Speaking of which, where can I reach you?"

Erin took out the card that Rhonda had made up for the company with Imagine That's logo, address and phone number on it. "You can reach me at work most of the time. Once in a while, I do go home, mostly to change my clothes," she confessed. "You have my home number already."

He tucked the card into the breast pocket of his smoke-gray suit jacket. "I'll call you soon," he told her.

Erin nodded as she left the office.

As he watched her turn down the hall and make her way to the elevator, Steve didn't turn around and go back to his office again. Instead he went in search of one of his senior partners. Specifically, he wanted to talk to the man who was responsible for his being with the firm in the first place. He had a proposition to make to the man that involved taking on a case pro bono for the first time in a long time.

"You want us to take a pro bono case?" Gerald Donnal asked, seeming somewhat surprised by the request.

Steve stood in the senior partner's office, making his case. "It's either that, sir, or I'm going to have to take some of that vacation time I've accrued in the past two years. At this point, I'm not sure just how much time I'm going to need to take."

Graying at the temples and widening around the waist, Gerald Donnal looked at him.

"Not that I don't think you richly deserve some time off, Steven, but isn't this rather sudden? And what does it have to do with a pro bono case?"

"Sudden, yes," Steve admitted—he was a little surprised at how quickly he'd made up his mind about her. He was the type who didn't accept half measures as "good enough." "And if you don't want to take this case pro bono," Steve continued, "then I need some time off so I can handle it on my own time."

"That important to you?" Donnal asked, clearly intrigued.

Steve was about to automatically deny the personal

aspect of the question but decided that maybe Donnal had a better take on it than he did. The old man certainly had a keener eye.

"In a word, yes," he told the senior partner.

"Then by all means, take the case pro bono," Donnal said. "If it's that important to you, then it's that important to us. I trust your judgment, boy," he assured him. "Now, if you don't mind, I have an appointment with a grieving widow to determine just how 'grieving' this woman actually is."

"I'll get out of your hair," Steve said, already walking toward the door. "And thanks."

Donnal laughed, waving away the words. "Don't mention it. You've brought in enough business for us to cut you a little slack. Hope this turns out as well as you think it will."

"Oh, it will, Mr. Donnal," he promised with enthusiasm. "I have a really good feeling about this and it will."

Chapter Twelve

Because he'd noted Erin's discomfort in his office and he wanted her to be at ease, when Steve asked to get together with her, he suggested going back to the café where they'd gone right after their Career Day presentations at Jason's class.

Rather than feel relaxed in the neutral setting, Erin was tense the moment she walked in and saw Steve already seated at a table.

He waved her over and as she crossed to him, she was convinced he'd chosen this public café as a meeting place because he was afraid she might be one of those women who caused a scene when she didn't receive the information she wanted.

"I took the liberty of getting the same thing for you that you ordered last time," he told her, indicating the coffee and turnover at her place setting.

Food was the furthest thing from her mind, despite the fact that she was surprised and touched that he even remembered what she'd had that day.

Taking a seat, she was about to tell him that she understood his deciding not to take the case when Steve told her, "The firm's agreed to take on your case pro bono."

Struck speechless for a moment, she managed to get out, "Really?"

He smiled at her. "Really."

And then she played back his words and apprehension burrowed through her. "The firm," she repeated. "But not you?"

He was quick to place her misunderstanding to rest. "Oh, definitely me," he assured her. "I'll be the one representing this case."

Before she allowed herself to breathe a sigh of relief, she had one last question to put to him. "Pro bono. Doesn't that mean that there'll be no charge?" she asked him.

"Yes."

Erin shook her head. As much as she needed this, she had to turn it down. Her self-esteem dictated it. "Thank you, but no."

"I don't understand," he told her.

"I'm desperate," she told him honestly, "but not *that* desperate." Her eyes met his. "I can't and won't accept charity." She was surprised and touched by his offer. But she didn't want to be in his debt. Still, the fact that he was actually offering to help gladdened her heart and managed to stir something within her that she told herself had no place here.

It stayed nonetheless.

"It's not charity, Erin," Steve insisted.

To her, charity had a very simple definition. "I'm not paying for your services, right?"

"Right," he was forced to admit. "But—"

She cut Steve off, not allowing him to finish. "If that isn't the definition of charity, then what would *you* call it?"

He never hesitated. "A fair trade. You told me that you go to the local hospitals on Christmas Eve and the first day of summer vacation to distribute those dinosaurs of yours, right?"

"Yes, but—"

"My helping you make this suit go away is to pay you back for that." He wouldn't be strictly honest with her if he didn't tell her the second part. "And also to give the firm a write-off."

That just proved her point. "In other words, charity," Erin concluded.

"By allowing my firm to represent you and casting us in a good light, you'd be doing us a favor and we in turn would be doing one for you by exposing this blackmailer in sheep's clothing," he told her. On the way over here he'd thought of an avenue of strategy to try. "You mentioned that you had gotten some favorable press from the father of one of the kids in the cancer ward and that was how your career took off, right?"

She looked at him, confused. Where was he going with this? "Yes, but—"

As he spoke, he leaned in over the table and closer to her, shutting out the rest of the world. Even with a table between them, she was acutely aware of him, of the cologne he was wearing. Of the way his eyes crinkled slightly at the edges.

"What do you think about getting in touch with him, letting him know about the case?" Steve proposed.

"Why would I do that?" she asked. "He was nice enough to get me the publicity I needed to make people aware of my product at the time. I don't want to repay him by asking him for another favor."

He struggled not to stare at her. Was this woman for real? In the world he lived in, the women he'd encountered of late were all devious and self-serving. She was like the antiversion of those women. She was single-handedly restoring his faith in humanity in general, and women in particular.

"My guess is that he would be more than happy to do something positive for you after you brought joy into his son's life. Not only that but this is the kind of human-interest story people respond to—altruism versus greed. It's the stuff that reputations and promotions are made of.

"And in the meantime, I think that I'll pay this Wade Baker a little visit after I get a few things straightened out first."

For the first time since Mike had told her about the suit against her company, Erin felt hopeful, which in turn ushered in just the slightest feeling of relief. She was very tempted to throw her arms around his neck and kiss him. But that, she knew, would open a door to a place she realized she was afraid to go.

So why was she dwelling on it the way she was?

Get a grip, Erin, she upbraided herself.

It didn't help, didn't change anything.

Her company was in trouble and here she was, fantasizing about the man who was offering to help. What was *wrong* with her?

"I don't know what to say," she told him.

Steve laughed. "Well, the words *thank you* come to mind."

She shook her head. "That doesn't seem nearly good enough."

He merely smiled at her. "It'll do for now."

"And later?" she asked, since that was what his tone indicated, that there'd be more to do down the line.

"Is later," he told her whimsically, adding a wink that went like an arrow straight into her stomach. She could feel her stomach tightening in anticipation— of what, she wasn't sure. Nevertheless, anticipation was still there, heightening all her senses and placing them all on red alert.

"Meanwhile," Steve continued as he finished the last of his turnover, "nothing's changed, right? We're still on for Sunday?"

She nodded in response. "I wouldn't miss it for the world," she told him.

"That's good." He'd said that with more than a little enthusiasm. Realizing that she might think he was pressuring her and thereby making her feel that he was in the same sort of category that Baker was, Steve was quick to add, "Because I would really hate to have to disappoint Jason."

Her eyes met his. The boy was not the first person who came to her mind when she thought about the possible cancellation of her date. But in order to keep this from progressing too rapidly or going down the wrong road, she murmured, "Same here," as she quickly lowered her eyes again.

Steve called A.J. Clarke the moment he returned to his office.

A.J. and his partner, George Matthews, had been his law firm's private investigators for the past five years. Both were excellent at what they did, but over time he had found A.J. to be the more approachable as well as flexible of the two.

"What's up?" A.J. asked as he closed the office door behind him and crossed to the chair in front of Steve's desk.

Steve got right down to it. "I need you to locate a Wade Baker for me. Not just where he lives but what his daily routine is. I want to find out where he works, who he interacts with. Does he have friends, or is he a loner? In short, I want a complete picture of Baker's current day-to-day life."

"You want a background check on him, as well?" A.J. asked.

Of average height, build and coloring, A.J. blended into the surrounding scenery better than anyone he had ever seen, which was in part what made the man so good at what he did. A.J. made no impression— except when he wanted to get up close and personal. Then the impression was *very* distinct. Despite his nondescript appearance, he was not a man to be taken lightly or dismissed.

Steve nodded. "Might not be a bad idea." Knowing how busy the investigator tended to be, he added, "And I need this done ASAP. It's for a case that needs to go away as quickly as possible."

Getting up, A.J. nodded. He began backing out of the office. "Consider it gone already."

It was well-known that A.J. made no promises he couldn't keep. "Knew I could count on you," Steve told the man with a satisfied smile.

"So should we start thinking about re-forming the company under a different logo?" Mike asked her the moment Erin walked back into their office.

The feeling growing inside her for the past forty minutes had been laced with optimism. She realized that she was putting her money on a positive outcome, but Steve really did make her feel that everything was going to be all right.

"I think we can hold off awhile on that," she told Mike.

"You ran Baker over with your car?" Neal asked hopefully.

"No. But I did manage to get a lawyer to represent us," she told the others. She opened the bottom drawer of her desk and dropped her purse into it.

"A lawyer?" Rhonda echoed.

"We can afford a lawyer?" Gypsy asked from the doorway, drawn into the room by the sound of voices.

"I thought you said we couldn't," Judith reminded her.

Turning around to face the administrative assistant, Erin corrected the misinformation before it began to escalate. "The lawyer's taking the case pro bono."

"Worked your magic on him, did you?" Mike's laugh made it clear that the question was a rhetorical one.

Gypsy was apparently still trying to untangle the information. "Bono's a lawyer?" she asked, confused, looking from Mike to Erin.

"Not Bono the singer, *bono,*" Erin emphasized, enunciating both the Irish singer's name and the Latin term.

Rhonda stepped up to explain the term to the administrative assistant. "It means that Erin got someone to work for free on our behalf."

"Just how did you manage that?" Christian asked.

"Remember that Career Day talk I gave at that elementary school the other day?" Erin asked.

"The one you almost didn't go to?" Mike recalled. "Yeah. What about it?"

"The other speaker that day was a lawyer," she told them, thinking that would answer any of their questions on the subject.

But clearly not for Mike. "And we want a lawyer who gives speeches to kindergartners?"

"Second graders," she corrected, then added with feeling, "And we want this one."

"Oh, so it's like that, is it?" Mike asked, smirking.

The expression on his face told her that he was clearly interested. His interest sparked the others', as well.

"It's not like anything, Mike," she insisted even though she wasn't nearly as certain about that as she tried to sound. There was something about Steve that managed to seep through all her self-constructed barriers, barriers that were supposed to keep her safe. "He's the only lawyer I know, so I called him to see if he had a suggestion or knew anyone who could help us get Wade to drop this stupid lawsuit. Steve wound up volunteering to help us, saying his company could do it pro bono because it needed a write-off."

"Do we get to meet him?" Neal asked, clearly very interested.

She could just see how that would go. There'd be six people talking at Steve, most likely all at once. He'd be running for the hills within minutes.

"And risk him deciding *not* to take the case?" she responded. "Not a chance."

"So when do we find out if it's okay to go on working here?" Mike asked.

"Steve said that we should just continue working the way we always have. In other words, just act as if everything was all right," she told them.

"Oh, so it's 'Steve' now, is it?" Neal asked with an extrawide smile. "Good for you, Erin."

She ignored Neal's obvious meaning and just zeroed in on his initial comment, answering it as if it had been serious.

"As far as I know, that's always been his name. Now let's get back to filling those orders or even if we win the case, we won't have a company to run, because we will have been forced to close our doors due to a failure to fill back orders. Understood?" she asked, looking from one person on the team to another.

It was Mike who spoke up first. "Understood, *mein Kapitän*." He saluted her, then turned toward the others. "You heard the lady, guys. We have dinosaurs to bring to life. Let's get cracking!"

Erin watched with a surge of emotion as everyone got busy and she silently prayed that Steve had a miracle in his bag of tricks. Otherwise, this would be a thing of the past all too soon.

The next day, no matter what else she was doing, Erin was aware that she lived for the phone. Or, more accurately put, she lived *to hear it ring* and bring her good news.

Each time it did ring, whether she was at work or at home, she would snatch up the receiver and the first thing out of her mouth was always his name.

By late afternoon, her nerves were frayed but she calculated that eventually, the odds had to be in her favor.

"Steve?"

There was a momentary pause on the other end of the line and then a deep male voice asked her, "How did you know it was me?"

Since she had picked up the landline's receiver on the first ring, he assumed that the caller ID hadn't had time to register yet. Was she just anticipating his call, or was there something more to it?

It was ludicrous to believe something like that, he told himself, and yet...

There was no "yet" and he couldn't allow his imagination to get carried away.

"Lucky guess," she answered evasively. The next

moment, she dropped any attempt at sounding non-chalant. They both knew how very important the correct outcome to this case was to her. "So, any news about my case?"

"It's progressing," was all Steve said in response. He would have loved to have told her that things looked as if they were going well on his end. If, for some reason, it all fell apart at the last minute, then she would be even more devastated, in his opinion, than she would be if she kept her expectations in check.

At this point, from the feedback he was getting from A.J., he felt fairly optimistic about the case's outcome. Apparently Wade Baker, the man suing Erin and her company, was more of a blackmailer than a wronged innovator. A.J. had told him that he was presently running down one very telling piece of information. Once that was verified, he could proceed with bringing about an end to the whole ordeal.

"I'm just calling to make sure that we're all set for tomorrow."

"I thought we already verified that."

"I never take anything for granted until it's actually happening."

"Well, you can take this for granted. I, for one, could really use the diversion," she told him.

He felt for her. She'd put her heart and soul into this company and now she found herself in a position where it could all come to an end through no fault of her own. He knew what it felt like to suddenly have the floor pulled out from under you, except unlike in the cartoons, the free fall came immediately, not when you finally looked down.

"It's going to be all right, Erin," he told her quietly, then went on to say in a more audible voice, "I can't tell you what a transformation there's been in Jason because of you and that dinosaur."

And it wasn't just in Jason's life but in mine, as well, he added silently.

Out loud, he said, "I'll pick you up tomorrow at ten if that's all right with you."

"That'll be perfect," she answered.

"So no full-time job to speak of?" Steve asked A.J. as he skimmed over the report that the investigator had brought him.

"None that I could find. Not since your client fired him six months ago." A.J. leaned back in the chair as he faced Steve. "He's gone from job to job. Three by my count. Currently, Baker's got this part-time gig as a night watchman at the Newport Beach outdoor mall. Not exactly brain surgery—especially since he's already been cited for sleeping on the job once.

"During the day, he gets together with a few guys he seems to be friendly with at The Main Space, this bar that's within walking distance—or stumbling distance—of his apartment," A.J. told him.

Steve looked at the array of candid shots the firm's investigator had taken of Baker. He felt as if he was looking at a wasted life.

Frowning, he glanced up at A.J. "He sounds like a real winner."

"It gets better," A.J. said. "Baker's been bragging

to some of his so-called friends that he's going to be coming into big money soon. He's really counting on this thing and he's not going to go away easily."

Steve had to ask, though he really didn't want to. The more he interacted with Erin, the more he found himself really liking her. He didn't want to hear anything that would make him change his mind about her.

But as her lawyer, he had to have all the facts first. "Anything to substantiate his claim about her stealing his idea?"

"I did some digging into both their personal lives," A.J. told him.

Steve suddenly felt as if the floor beneath his feet had turned into a web of pins and needles. "And?"

"Your client's got a spotless reputation. Couldn't find *anyone* who had a bad word to say about her. It was like trying to find someone to bad-mouth Mother Teresa. The guy, however, is another story. Seems he tried to blackmail a woman he was actually having an affair with, threatened to tell her husband after things fell apart between them and she gave him his walking papers."

"What happened?"

"Interesting story. She came clean to her husband. He forgave her, called the police and had Baker arrested. Charges were eventually dropped in exchange for Baker's promise never to come near either of them again. This is not his first rodeo," A.J. concluded. "You want me to have a talk with him, tell him what he's facing if he goes through with this?" the investigator offered.

"Thanks, but I think I'll handle it from here," Steve

told him, then smiled when he saw the skeptical expression in the other man's eyes. "Not my first rodeo, either." He let the report drop back on his desk as he looked at the investigator sitting opposite him. He knew how busy both he and his partner were. "Thanks for getting to this so quick."

A.J. shrugged away his words. "You don't usually put a rush on things. I figured that this had to be important."

Steve glanced down at the report. He thought of the fear he'd seen in Erin's eyes when she told him about the suit. "It is."

A.J. ventured a guess. "Personal?"

Rather than deny it, Steve smiled, wondering what had initially given him away. "What makes you ask that?"

The investigator spread his hands as if the answer was self-evident. "Hey, I'm an investigator."

Steve smiled. "This client is too much of a lady to know how to fight dirty. She's one of those people who would never dream of hurting anyone or of lying and isn't able to understand why anyone else would do that. I was pretty certain that the suit was baseless, but I also felt that it would be hard for her to prove. I just wanted to make absolutely sure that there was nothing to the guy's claim—or anything that he could effectively twist to support his accusation."

A.J. took his cue and rose from his seat. "Glad I could help. Oh, and if your 'client' could see her way clear to it, my five-year-old loves dinosaurs and would be thrilled to have one of the ones she makes. The one in the cowboy hat," he specified. When Steve looked at him in surprise, A.J.'s grin widened again. "Like I said, I'm an investigator."

Steve laughed, nodding at him. "So you are, A.J., so you are. I'll talk to her," he promised.

"Good enough for me. And if you change your mind about having that talk with that lowlife, my offer still stands."

Steve nodded again. "I'll keep that in mind," he promised. But this was something he looked forward to doing himself.

Steve debated getting the confrontation with Baker over with as soon as possible. Erin deserved to know, one way or the other, if she actually had anything to worry about.

But if something unforeseen happened or the confrontation with Baker turned ugly, he would rather not have to tell Erin before they went to the movies tomorrow. He didn't want to take a chance on ruining the day for his son—or for him, for that matter.

This was the first so-called date he was going on where not only was his son included, which was unusual in itself, but the woman he was going out with had actually *asked* to have his son come along. That, to him, was extraordinary.

Each time he had made the suggestion to include his son to any of the other women he had seen previously, the woman either quickly changed the subject or seemed disappointed and the idea of their going out on a date at all died very quickly on the vine.

No one wanted to acknowledge that obvious truth. That he and Jason were a package deal.

That was, no one wanted to acknowledge it until Erin had come along.

He wanted to give their date a fighting chance to flourish before he was forced to factor in any extraneous occurrences.

Steve supposed that made him sound selfish.

On the other hand, that also made him sound like a father.

Chapter Thirteen

"Do you think he'll be there?" Jason asked.

Steve didn't have to glance up in his rearview mirror to know that the boy was fidgeting behind him in the car seat. He could tell from the sound of his son's voice. Nonetheless, he raised his gaze to the mirror to make eye contact.

"Do I think who'll be there?" he asked the boy.

"Tex," Jason said impatiently, as if his father should have known that. "Do you think he'll be at Erin's house? Does he live with her? And the other dinosaurs, the ones she brought with her to my classroom—do you think they live with her, too? Or do they all have their own house?"

"All good questions," Steve told his son. "None of which I know the answer to." Those were all questions he felt Erin was best equipped to field.

He made a right turn at the next corner. He'd programmed his GPS before leaving the house, but he'd gone over the route several times the old-fashioned way—on a road map he kept in his car in case of emergencies. Even the most sophisticated of electronics had been known to malfunction on occasion. Paper, however, never did. Whenever possible, he liked having a sure thing in his corner.

"But we'll be there very soon," he told Jason, "so you can ask her yourself."

As far as the boy was concerned, he had already decided the answer to his first question was going to be yes. Now taking it as a given, Jason continued on from there. "Do you think she'll bring Tex with her when we go to the movies?"

"Another question you can ask her," Steve told his son.

It wasn't so much that he was buck passing as he was setting the stage for his son to interact with Erin. He had to admit that he liked seeing the two of them together. It reinforced his feelings that he was on the right track with this woman.

"Tex Jr. wants to talk to his dad," Jason declared out of the blue.

Steve smiled to himself. He took that to be another sign of the progress he'd made in his son's life— thanks to Erin and her dinosaur.

"That's always a good thing," he said. "Fathers and sons *should* talk. Oh, there's her house just up ahead," he pointed out.

Jason cocked his head as he regarded the two-story structure. "It looks like a regular house," his son observed.

Steve heard the disappointment in the boy's voice. "Well, that's because it's been disguised."

"Disguised?" Jason echoed, perking up.

"Uh-huh. This way people don't know that's where the dinosaurs live and they don't try to bother those dinosaurs. Otherwise, Tex and his friends would *never* get any rest."

It took a moment for the boy to digest what he'd been told. And then he looked up as if everything all fell into place for him. He grinned broadly.

"Oh."

My God, Steve thought, he was making things up on the spur of the moment. Maybe being around Erin was rubbing off on him. He found he rather liked the idea.

Steve had just barely pulled up to the curb when Jason began begging, "Undo me, Dad. Undo me! Quick!" he pleaded.

"Hold your horses, fella. I've got to come to a full stop first," he told his son.

"The car's stopped, it's stopped!" Jason all but shouted excitedly. "Tex Jr. wants to see his dad, like now!"

Steve got out and opened the rear-passenger door and began to undo the restraints on his son's car seat. Maybe he had somehow oversold this whole thing. He wanted the boy to be prepared—just in case.

"You know, we're not sure about Tex yet, Jason. He might not be there," he warned his son.

Jason's face fell about as far as a small face could. "Where's he gonna be, Dad?"

Steve said the first thing that came into his head. "Well, he might have gone to the park. Dinosaurs like parks," Steve added for good measure, as if that would settle the dispute.

Working on the car-seat restraints, he saw his son's eyes grow huge as he looked at something behind him.

"No, he didn't, Dad!" Jason cried. "Look! He's right there!"

Turning around, Steve saw Erin walking out of her house. In her arms she was holding the dinosaur. The woman had a sixth sense, he thought gratefully.

"Right on time," Tex declared, nodding at his son and him. The dinosaur turned his head to look at the woman carrying him. "Told you they'd be here on time," the T. rex said to Erin.

Erin inclined her head as she smiled at the duo. "I told Tex I thought you might be late," she explained.

"Dad was being slow, but I made him hurry up," Jason told her. Still strapped in, he leaned against the restraints, completely focused on the dinosaur in Erin's arms. "Is Tex coming with us?" Jason asked hopefully.

"I sure am. Wild horses couldn't keep me away." Holding the toy, Erin had the dinosaur lean in toward the car. "And I see you brought Tex Jr. with you. Has he been behaving?"

"Uh-huh," Jason answered, solemnly nodding his head up and down.

Erin's eyes met Steve's. The next moment, a warm

feeling infused itself within her. "Just let me get my purse and lock the front door," she told him. "I'll be right back."

The second she turned away, Jason bounced up and down in his car seat. "She's bringing him, Dad. She's bringing Tex! I told you she would," Jason cried, pleased beyond words.

"That you did," Steve agreed, seeing no reason to point out that Jason had voiced uncertainty about that outcome only a few minutes ago.

But Erin had that effect on people, he decided. Bringing out the positive in them.

In an incredibly short amount of time, she had become what amounted to a shining beacon in his son's life and no matter what else transpired, he was always going to be grateful to her for that.

Even though he had decided to set his sights on more.

"All set," Erin declared, returning back to his vehicle. Her hand on the shotgun seat's door handle, she took one glance at the little boy's hopeful expression and reconsidered her choice of seating arrangements. "You know, I'm going to ride in the back with Jason and Tex Jr. if you don't mind," she told Steve.

Getting in, she set Tex over to one side as she proceeded to rebuckle the straps on Jason's car seat that Steve had previously begun to undo.

Steve had taken in the same hopeful expression on his son's face, then seen the look of joy that had washed over him when Erin had said she'd decided to sit in the back with him.

She was one in a million, he thought.

"I don't mind at all," he said, then mouthed the words *thank you* to her.

The smile he received in return told him she'd heard him loud and clear.

Maybe one in *two* million, he amended silently as he started up his car again.

The movie lasted an hour and forty-two minutes but still seemed to just fly by. Before they knew it, they were filing out of the theater again.

Not wanting to see the date come to an end so soon, Steve heard himself suggesting getting lunch in one of the small restaurants that were scattered around the theater complex in the outdoor mall.

"Unless you're pressed for time," he felt bound to add on, just in case she felt that she had more than done her duty in sitting through over an hour and a half of an animated movie about a wise-cracking hero with a magic carpet that always flew to his rescue. He wanted her to feel she had a way out if she wanted it.

Erin didn't have to look down to know that Steve's son was holding his breath, waiting for a positive answer from her. She didn't want the boy suffocating himself, so she quickly responded, "I've decided to declare today a work-free day."

The next moment, Jason did his best imitation of a jumping jack, all while shouting his mealtime preference. "Pizza!" Jason cried. "Me and Tex Jr. want pizza." He looked from his father to Erin, searching for backup.

"Tex Jr. and I," she gently corrected.

"You, too?" the boy exclaimed, delighted. "That makes three of us, Dad."

Erin opened her mouth to take another stab at correcting the boy's grammar, then decided just to go along with it for now. With luck, there would be another time when she could play the grammarian.

"Most likely four," she told Jason, "because Tex likes pizza, too."

"Hear that, Dad?" Jason asked, his eyes beaming as he turned toward his father.

"I sure do," Steve answered, but he was looking at Erin as he said it. Looking at her and thinking that getting roped into Career Day had probably been one of the luckiest unplanned incidents of his life. "I guess that's unanimous, then."

"What's u-nan-i, um, u-nan-i—that word, Dad?" Jason asked, giving up trying to pronounce the word.

"It means we all agree," Erin told the boy. "And that's a good thing."

That was all that Jason needed. "Yeah!" he crowed. "Pizza for everybody!"

Without thinking, strictly reacting, Erin hugged the boy to her.

Jason glowed.

"I don't think I've ever seen him actually get completely worn out before," Steve confessed some seven and a half hours later, his voice barely above a whisper. He was talking about Jason. His son had literally fallen asleep on the sofa midsentence, explaining something about a video game he and Erin were playing—a creative video game that tested the player's memory rather than his reflexes to see how quickly he could eliminate an ongoing alien threat. The game, involving a group of friendly dinosaurs based on her creations, had been at Erin's suggestion. Her company was thinking of marketing the game in the near future. Jason was thrilled to be her test subject.

"Well, considering that he's been on the go from early this morning, I figured that eventually he'd have to run out of steam—even overactive kids get tired," she told Steve. Then, seeing that her last comment didn't draw any agreement from him, she asked, "Didn't you ever get tired when you were a kid?"

Steve shook his head. "I really don't remember much from back then."

"Really?" She had just assumed that he would have been able to recall events and feelings he'd gone through as a boy.

"Really," he assured her.

"That's a shame," she said. Without that to tap into, empathy for certain things his son was going through would be difficult for Steve. "Some of my fondest memories go back to my childhood."

"I guess that's pretty lucky for the rest of the kids," he commented, thinking of the toys she'd created. "And me," he added significantly, thinking of what she had managed to achieve with Jason. He looked down at his sleeping son now and smiled. It had been a good day for the Kendall men. "I guess that I'd better get him up to bed."

"Would you mind if I helped?" she asked.

Steve watched her for a long moment, then smiled. "I think I'd like that."

Preceding her on the stairs, Steve carried Jason up to the boy's room and laid him down on the bed. Erin untied the laces on Jason's sneakers and then slipped them off slowly so as not to wake him. She placed them next to the bed.

Out of the corner of her eye, she saw Steve taking a pair of pajamas out of the bureau's top drawer. On impulse, she offered a suggestion.

"Why don't you just cover him with a blanket? If you start undressing him, Jason might wake up." She smiled fondly at the boy. "There's nothing wrong with sleeping in your clothes. Waking up dressed is kind of fun at Jason's age."

"Something else you remember?" he asked her, the pajamas half in his hand, half still in the drawer.

She nodded. "That's why I'm making the suggestion," she told him.

"Okay, then leaving Jason in his clothes it is," Steve declared agreeably, the corners of his mouth curving as he put the pajamas back and slipped a blanket over his son's small body. The boy was going to get a kick out of this when he woke up tomorrow, Steve thought.

"Almost forgot the most important part," Erin suddenly said. Before he could ask her what that was, she had slipped Tex Jr., his stuffed dinosaur, in under the covers with the boy.

Backing away from the bed, Erin took in the peaceful picture that they had created.

Her expression was unreadable, Steve thought.

Prodded by his curiosity, he couldn't resist asking, "What are you thinking?"

"Just that I thought I'd have a couple of these myself by now," she admitted.

"You mean kids?"

She nodded her head. "Yes." Smiling, she gazed up at him. "Short people."

"You're not exactly over-the-hill," Steve pointed out.

She inclined her head. She'd heard all the excuses before. "I know, I know, but there are these pesky little details in the way."

Leaving the light on in Jason's room, Steve eased the door closed behind them. His curiosity further aroused, he continued their conversation in the hallway. "Pesky details?" he repeated.

"Yes, finding someone, falling in love with him— having him fall in love with me," she enumerated. "Then, of course, there's that last really big, scary step to take."

Intrigued, he just kept feeding her questions as they went down the stairs. "Which is?"

She even took a breath before saying the answer. "Getting married."

"It doesn't have to be a scary step." It hadn't been in his judgment. To him it had just been the most natural progression of things.

"Easy for you to say," she scoffed. "You've already gone through it."

"I wasn't exactly born married," he countered. Then a thought suddenly occurred to him. "Haven't you ever been in love, Erin?"

Erin pressed her lips together, again debating not saying anything. He'd probably think she was some sort of a freak if she told him the truth.

Stalling for time until an idea came to her, she asked, "Honestly?"

It had never occurred to him that she could be anything but. "Sure."

With a sigh, she murmured, "Then no," as she looked away.

Or tried to. With the crook of his finger beneath her chin, Steve turned her head until she was facing him again.

"Never?" he questioned incredulously.

She was right. He did think there was something wrong with her. She tried to turn it into a joke. "Does Batman count?"

"How old were you?" he asked.

"Almost eleven," she told him.

At that age, she was forming the woman she was going to be in a few short years. No one believed in comic-book superheroes at that age.

"Then no," he said, suppressing a laugh. Then he said a touch more seriously, "Maybe you just never went out with the right person."

She glanced away again. "And maybe I never went out at all."

That really brought him up short. For a second, he was certain he hadn't heard her correctly.

"What?"

How did she explain this without coming off like a complete dork? She decided just to admit the truth, without any embellishments or excuses. *Just the facts, ma'am,* as they used to say by way of a joke in some program or other she'd seen.

"After I got well and left the hospital, I felt as if I had fallen hopelessly behind socially and every other way. I tried to catch up but, well—" she raised her shoulders again in a helpless gesture "—I wasn't exactly stellar at mingling or getting along with other people my own age for the most part. Somehow, the experience I'd had made me out of sync with the world. That's probably another reason why I got involved with making more copies of Tex and the other dinosaurs that came after him. Doing that helped to fill a real void in my life. The dinosaurs were like my alter egos, my friends, if you will. I'd wind up talking to the dinosaurs and pouring out my heart to them when no one was around," she confessed.

He didn't understand. The woman he'd just spent the day with was warm and giving and, above all, fun. He'd seen her interacting with the people she worked with and there was no sign of the socially awkward woman she claimed to be.

"But what about those people you work with? You said they were your friends in college and I'm sure you get along well with them. If I was a betting man, I'd say they would all gladly go to the mat for you. That's a wrestling term that means they'd do anything for you," he explained.

She smiled. "I know what that means. And as for the way we get along, it's *because* they're my friends that we get along so well. I never dated any of the guys. That was just a given. We care about each other like family."

He approached what she was claiming from another angle. "Okay, while I can accept that all of you are just really good friends, nothing more, I'm finding it very hard to believe that someone as beautiful as you never got involved with anyone."

"I'm not beautiful."

"Yes, you are," Steve insisted. When she opened her mouth to protest, he stressed, "Inside as well as out." Because his emotions felt as if they were all colliding within him, he experienced a moment of weakness and allowed himself to caress her face. "If I had met you under different circumstances…" His voice trailed off as he struggled with a very real frustration.

"What?" Erin whispered, her eyes held prisoner by his. "If you had met me under different circumstances, what?" she asked him.

"If I had met you under different circumstances, I would be very tempted to kiss you right now. But you're my client," he told her, forcing himself to drop his hand to his side, "so I can't."

But she wasn't so ready to back away. Something was going on inside of her, something that she didn't want to back away from just yet.

"Would kissing me jeopardize my case?"

The words felt dry on his tongue. "No, but—"

She'd wondered on occasion what she was missing, but she'd wondered only in the absolute sense because there had never actually been anyone she had wanted to kiss or be kissed by.

Until now.

Drawing her courage to her, she heard herself saying, "Then what's stopping you?"

"It's a matter of ethics," he said, though it was growing increasingly difficult for him to remain steadfast to those principles. Not when she was here like this before him, tempting every fiber of his being. Making him remember that he was more than just a father, a son, a lawyer. That beneath it all, he was still a man with a man's desires.

"But if I said it was all right?" she asked, her voice barely an audible whisper. "Then would you kiss me?"

Technically, with or without her permission, it wasn't all right. But there was more than just technicalities at play here. There was a connection he'd all but given up hope of ever finding or having again. A connection that seemed to have evolved of its own accord, through no effort on his part.

If he let this moment, this chance to explore what *could* be, pass, he might never be able to go back and recapture it. Recapture what he felt was something rare and precious. Something filled with such endless possibilities.

As much as he wanted to go forward, Steve put the next move in her court.

"Do you want me to?" he asked.

Her heart was hammering so hard in her chest Erin was surprised that he didn't hear it—or, at the very least, that it hadn't just fallen out at his feet. Because he owned it, free and clear.

Her eyes still riveted to his, she gave him her answer. The only answer she could.

She uttered a breathless "Yes."

Chapter Fourteen

As his fingers gently slid along her cheeks, then slipped into her hair, Erin went with the moment as he brought his mouth down to hers.

And braced herself.

Her pulse accelerated as Steve deepened the kiss layer by layer until she had gotten completely lost in him. Completely consumed by her need for him.

Her head spinning, Erin dug her fingertips into his shoulders, desperately trying to anchor herself to something solid so that she wasn't embarrassed by her knees suddenly buckling beneath her. Her knees began to feel like mush and were swiftly losing the ability to support her at all.

She was utterly enveloped by this incredible sensation throbbing all through her. A sensation that was every bit as wondrous and wonderful as she'd once fantasized it would be.

Was this what it was all about? The excitement, the meeting of two souls that belonged together? She'd just resigned herself to making toys that brought out the best in children, that made children—children she was never going to have—happy. Joy on *this* level was something she had given up all hope of ever finding, of ever being allowed to experience.

Thank God she'd been wrong.

Standing up higher on her toes, feeling as if she were literally free-falling in space, she clung to Steve and the inflammatory kiss they were sharing for all she was worth. Her body was frantically heating, urging her not to stop, urging her to continue because this—whatever *this* actually was—might never come her way again.

He had to stop, Steve ordered himself, stop before he completely lost the ability to think, to exercise control over the desires that were, even now, wrapping him up in thin, steely bands and taking him prisoner.

With more effort than he'd ever had to employ in this sort of a situation before, he placed his hands on Erin's shoulders and pulled his head back, away from her.

The look of confusion and desolation in her eyes almost drew him back in but he managed to keep a tight rein on the scrambling shreds of his emotions.

It took him several seconds to find his voice. "I'll get my neighbor to stay with Jason and then I'll take you home."

She wanted the ground to open up beneath her

feet and just swallow her whole. How could a human being go from bordering on ecstasy to feeling this hollow, this empty, in the space of a nanosecond?

Even though she felt like just disappearing and putting this behind her, she had to know, had to ask, otherwise this would haunt her for as long as she could form a coherent thought.

"Did I do something wrong?"

The question stunned him. Was that what she thought? How could she?

"Wrong?" he echoed incredulously, staring at her in utter awe. "Oh, God, no. If you had done it any more right, I wouldn't have been able to dynamite myself away from you."

That cleared up nothing. If anything, it just confused her more. "Then why are you taking me home?"

"Because this—" he waved his hand in a circle between their two bodies "—can't happen between us."

But why? her mind screamed. "You don't want it to?"

For a man who made his living by speaking succinctly and getting to the heart of the matter, he was really doing a terrible job right now, where it counted the most, he reproached himself.

"What I *don't* want is for you to look back and regret this."

Was that it? Was he afraid he was seducing her? Stripping her of her own free will? He couldn't have been more wrong.

"The only thing I'm going to regret," she told him, enunciating every syllable carefully, "is if you send me home now."

He wanted to believe that with his entire being, but he couldn't let himself. "You don't know what you're saying."

She pulled herself together as best she could, cloaking herself in her dignity.

"I'm not drugged or drunk. I know *exactly* what I'm saying. After a certain point, when it *didn't* happen to me, I thought that all those stories about walking on air, about a million emotions swirling all through you, making your head spin and your knees weak, weren't really true. Or if they were, they weren't true for me.

"One of the reasons that Wade became so furious with me was because I wouldn't sleep with him. I rejected him because when he tried to kiss me, I didn't want him to. I didn't *feel* anything when I was near him."

She looked at him meaningfully. "It was different with you. I did feel something. And then you kissed me and instead of being let down, I was lifted up. Up to a level I'd never even dreamed about before. So unless you're regretting this, please don't send me—"

She didn't get a chance to finish, because just as before, he slipped his hands along her face, except that this time, the kiss didn't begin slowly and then, inch by inch, blossom.

This time, the passion, the desire, they were all there right from the start, knocking down any barriers, any walls that might have been erected on some other plane.

And as he kissed Erin, as he allowed the passion that had been so hopelessly locked away and dormant within him for these past two years to explode, she leaned into him. And he just *knew* she was absorbing every vibration, every nuance, every tidal wave of desire and emotion that he was sharing with her.

Clinging to him, feeling the wild pounding of her heart, Erin was vaguely aware that the floor beneath her feet wasn't there anymore. When the shock of that registered and then subsided, she realized that she hadn't been catapulted into some other stratosphere. Instead Steve had lifted her into his arms and was now carrying her toward the stairs.

Hardly able to breathe, she still managed to draw her head back just for a fraction of a moment.

He thought for a second that she'd had a change of heart. But the next moment, the wide smile and starry look in her eyes told him otherwise.

"How did you know?" she asked in a low whisper, the words feathering with her warm breath along his neck, causing his excitement to heighten.

"Know what?"

"That my favorite passage in *Gone with the Wind* was when Rhett carries Scarlett up the stairs. I read it over and over again a dozen times," she admitted.

Not wanting to ruin the moment entirely by saying he'd had no idea she was enamored by the scene, he smiled into her eyes and said, "Lucky guess."

He could, in the heat of the moment, be forgiven for telling the white lie instead of revealing that he had to climb the stairs because his bedroom was on the second floor.

As a bachelor, this wild feeling pounding in his veins would have had him taking her right there in

the living room. But as a father, a certain protec-
tiveness took precedence over desire, no matter how
red-hot and demanding that desire might be or how
overwhelming the rush of sensations was.

His lips were covering hers again before he reached
the landing. She was making him crazy, he couldn't
help thinking. But crazy in a good way.

Once inside his room, Steve pushed the door
closed with his back, then set her down, allowing
her feet to touch the floor rather than laying her on
his bed. Every single step of the way, he wanted to
give her the option of changing her mind and calling
a stop to what was happening, though he fervently
prayed that she wouldn't.

But when she clung to him like that, her lips fever-
ishly responding to his, igniting him, they still wound
up on his bed less than two heartbeats later. He had
no idea how they'd even gotten there, whether he was
the one who'd led the way or if she was responsible
for drawing him over there.

The dance was mutual.

He was far from inexperienced, but the lovemak-
ing that followed still took his breath away.

Erin responded to every pass of his hand, to every
kiss his lips pressed against her increasingly denuded
body. Each time he touched her, each time he kissed
her, he managed to ratchet up his own response to
her until he was fairly certain that between the two
of them, they could very easily wind up setting the
bed on fire—and probably not realize it.

It was the closest thing to an out-of-body experience she had ever had.

Nothing, *nothing* she had ever felt could even come close to this. There were things happening inside of her, desires, wants, emotions, raw sensations, she couldn't even begin to label or identify.

All she knew was that she wanted this wild madness to go on for as long as humanly possible. She didn't care that this was much further than she had ever gone before—or that she had ever *wanted* to go before. At this single moment in time, she *craved* to know what it felt like to belong to someone, be one with someone, for however long that physical union lasted.

Up to this point, she'd never cared one way or the other that she belonged to a very small group of people who had never physically made love with anyone.

But now she wanted to leave all that behind, because she had found a man she wanted to belong to, for however short a time he wanted her. She knew making love wasn't some silent, flowery pledge nailed to the word *forever.* This was about pleasure—and caring on her part, because if she hadn't cared, cared *deeply,* none of this would have happened.

Her whole body was damp with sweat and throbbing wildly with anticipation when Steve finally slid her beneath him and loomed over her, balancing his weight on his hands. Lowering himself slowly, he sealed his mouth to hers first, and then he entered her.

The very next moment, as the shock registered, he stopped.

She saw his eyes fly open, saw the utter surprise within them. Knew in her heart that the next second, it would all stop. All be over.

She couldn't bear that to happen, so she raised her hips to his insistently, moving so that whatever his good intentions might have been, they hadn't a prayer of triumphing over the lure of her body.

The pain that shot through her when he pushed forward into her faded almost as quickly as it had materialized. The heat, the desire, the emotions all returned tenfold, seizing her and taking her to a place that she, however briefly, made her own—because he was there, as well.

His hips moved faster and faster and she kept pace with the rhythm, eager to reach the place he had been to so many times before—but never with her.

Until now.

When it finally exploded, enveloping her, the sensation she experienced was beyond anything she might have anticipated. Erin eagerly let the euphoria completely drench her as she clung to it.

Because she knew that the moment she returned back to earth, there would be questions to answer—and worse than that, his disappointment to face. With an almost superhuman effort, she attempted to seal herself off, even as she knew in her heart that it wasn't possible.

She returned to earth soundlessly.

The silence that echoed in the room grew louder and louder until she couldn't bear it anymore.

Turning toward Steve, she almost begged, "Say something."

"I don't know what to say." Raising himself up on his elbow, he looked at her, remorse etched into every inch of his chiseled face. "I'm sorry."

A moment ago she was wrapped in euphoria. Now she just felt horribly naked and exposed.

"I didn't mean to disappoint you," she said, turning away, fervently wishing that her clothes were close by instead of so far away on the floor.

Her words of apology ricocheted in his head. "Wait. What?"

How many ways did he want her to say it? "I know that if you'd known that I hadn't…done this before—" each word felt as if it weighed a ton as it left her lips "—you wouldn't have made love with me."

"No, I wouldn't have," he agreed, "at least, not like this."

It was Erin's turn to be confused again. "Like this?" she echoed. Then he *would* have made love to her, just under different circumstances? Was that what he was saying? She felt as if her brain was addled.

He searched for a better way to say it. He owed her at least that much for taking away so cavalierly something so precious.

"A first time is supposed to be memorable," he told her, "not just a spur-of-the-moment thing or—"

She put her fingers to his lips to stop his rambling apology. He didn't understand, did he?

"A first time is supposed to be with someone I wanted it to be with," she corrected.

He stared at her for a long moment, trying to absorb what she was saying to him. "You mean to tell me that I'm the first one—the first one that you've ever *wanted* to be with?"

"Yes, I thought you understood what I was saying before." The reason for his discomfort dawned on her. He was afraid she was going try to tie him down. "But you don't have to worry," she told him. "I'm not going to be turning up at your doorstep with wedding rings or invitations or—"

She didn't get to finish because, for the second time that evening, his lips took her words away from her as he covered her mouth with his own.

For one wild, heady moment, Erin allowed herself to get lost in his kiss. Then, drawing her head back, she asked, "Does this mean you forgive me?"

He smiled into her eyes. "What do you think?"

She could feel her own smile blossoming inside of her. "I think I have a lot to learn."

"Not nearly as much as you think. You have a great deal of natural talent to tap into." And then he grew serious as he looked at her. "But you really should have told me, you know."

She lifted one bare shoulder in a half shrug. "Not exactly the kind of topic a woman who does dinosaur voices can raise at the dining-room table."

"True enough," he told her, lightly skimming his fingertips along her face, moving her hair back out of her eyes. The next moment, moved by a fresh wave of desire, he lowered his lips to hers again.

The moment he did, the fire returned, igniting within his chest, his loins, his desire for her coming back with a vengeance as if it hadn't just been sated a scarce few minutes ago.

Steve had no idea what exactly it was about this woman that created such a fever in his blood, but he knew at this moment that the search he had suspended, the one that he'd hoped would yield not just

a partner for him but, just as importantly, a mother
for Jason, was not going to need to be revisited and
resurrected anytime in the near—or distant—future.

He'd found the woman he had been looking for.
All he'd had to do, he realized with a touch of irony,
was stop looking.

Now, of course, it got a little more complicated.
Now he had to find a way for her to *want* to be his
and remain his.

One step at a time, he cautioned himself as he
went on to make love with her. *One slow, deliberate
step at a time.*

Chapter Fifteen

"He's kind of a boring guy," A.J. informed Steve. After two weeks of surveillance, the private investigator had worked up Wade Baker's schedule and now placed it on Steve's desk. "One day is pretty much like another. For the most part, it almost looks like his part-time job interferes with his real vocation in life—drinking."

Steve turned the schedule around so he could examine it more carefully. There was little variation from one day to the next except for the weekends, when the man appeared to open the bar as well as close it down.

Why had Erin even hired Baker in the first place? She must have seen something in the man but for the life of him, he certainly didn't see it.

"This is just a hunch, but since you had me draw

up this guy's itinerary, I get the feeling that you don't want to waste precious time and resources fighting his suit in the court. You want to have some sense talked into the guy in person."

"Valid hunch," Steve granted.

A.J. nodded his head. "If you want, I could go to his place of work or that bar, have a talk with Baker, tell him that it might be in his best interest to back off before you make certain things public."

Steve seriously considered A.J.'s offer for exactly five seconds. Ordinarily, he wouldn't have even thought twice about the matter. Confrontations outside the courtroom or boardroom were something that he felt were A.J.'s purview.

"Thanks and no offense, but this one I want to handle personally," he told the detective.

"None taken," A.J. assured him. "But what if this guy wants to take a swing at that pretty face of yours? People get nervous if their lawyer shows up to represent their interest sporting a black eye."

He supposed if someone looked at the two of them, A.J. was the one who appeared as if he could handle himself in a situation. However, he wasn't exactly a novice in this department. He'd gotten in an altercation or two—and won—despite the expensive suits he wore.

"I didn't spend my years in college with my head constantly buried in a book. I can take care of myself if need be," he assured the investigator. "But thanks for the concern."

A.J. inclined his head. "Well, you know how to reach me if you need backup or change your mind."

In response, Steve patted the pocket where he kept his cell phone. "Yeah, I do."

Rather than go to Wade Baker's apartment or his place of work, Steve decided to do a little surveillance himself. So he went to the bar A.J. had said he frequented.

Sitting at a table for one over in the corner that was bathed in shadow, Steve nursed a beer for the better part of two hours until, apparently out of money and out of friends, the man he was observing decided to boisterously call it a night.

Steve walked behind the man for the two and a half blocks that existed between the bar and Baker's third-floor walk-up.

Just before the man got his keys out to unlock the main door that led into the tiny foyer and the stairs to his studio apartment, Steve tapped him on the shoulder.

Taking no chances, Baker turned around prepared to swing. Ready for him, Steve instantly pushed the other man back, slamming Baker's torso up against the wall.

Trapped between the wall and the hold Steve had on him, his face pressed against the building's aged brick exterior, Baker frantically protested, "Hey, buddy, if you're looking to mug me, it's your unlucky day. I'm tapped out. The bar's got all my money."

Steve was in no hurry to release him. Keeping him like this against the wall was also a way to keep his own anger in check. Because for two cents, he'd turn the man around and make him pay for intimidating Erin.

"I'm not looking to mug you, you sorry piece of wasted flesh. I'm looking to give you a warning. Just one," Steve told him, his voice coldly menacing. "Stay away from Erin O'Brien. Don't call her, don't see her. Don't text, Tweet, email or even so much as *think* about her. Because if you do, if you try to have any contact with her whatsoever, I'll have you thrown in jail on blackmail charges so fast you'll get whiplash."

Furious as well as frustrated, Baker snarled, "You can't prove anything!"

Steve spun Baker around to face him, making sure he kept a tight hold on his shirt collar. The man's complexion grew considerably redder.

"Oh, but I can, and I will. Especially since this isn't your first go-round with blackmail charges." Steve's eyes narrowed. "You're not nearly as clever as you think you are."

"Who the hell are you?" Baker demanded.

Steve took his time answering, continuing to grasp Baker's collar, keeping him in place. "I'm the guy who's got a whole file of sworn statements signed by people willing to testify that Erin created all those dinosaur characters her company manufactures long before she ever knew you. So if you know what's good for you and you value your health, you will forget you ever knew Erin O'Brien. As of *now,*" Steve emphasized.

There was a line of perspiration along the man's forehead, but he didn't go down easily. "Or what?" he challenged.

Steve had always been good at reading people, at detecting their small tells that allowed him to see beneath the facades they tried to maintain. It wasn't difficult for him to ascertain that Wade Baker was a coward. The other man got his way only by intimidating people who were weaker and smaller than he was. Any sort of threat from someone his own size or slightly bigger—which, fortunately, he was, Steve noted—had him backing off. It was only a matter of time—and not much time, at that.

Now, Steve was willing to bet, was no exception.

"Or I'll make you regret the day you were born," he told Baker evenly. "I'm serious about getting you tossed in jail on blackmail charges—if there's anything left of you after we have our little one-on-one 'discussion.'" He allowed his words to sink in before continuing. "Now, first thing tomorrow morning, you're calling your cousin, that shyster lawyer, and you're telling him that you've decided to change your mind. You're dropping the suit against Erin O'Brien and her company, Imagine That. Do I make myself clear?" he asked. When Baker didn't respond instantly, Steve got in his face. "Well, do I?"

"Yeah, yeah," Baker managed to croak out. "Perfectly clear."

With a look of sheer disgust, Steve released his grip on the other man's collar. Baker stumbled to the side, then darted into the foyer and ran up the stairs, presumably all the way up to his apartment.

Steve smiled to himself as he walked back the two and a half blocks to where he'd left his vehicle parked right outside the bar.

Sometimes, he thought, it felt good to get physical and get his hands a little dirty. He hadn't fully appreciated that until just now.

This time, as she stepped off the elevator on the floor where Steve's law firm was located, she didn't feel like an impostor. Didn't feel in the least bit nervous. She felt as if she were floating on air.

It hadn't even occurred to her that Steve might not be in his office until just now. Oh, she knew she could have just picked up her phone and called him about this new, unexpected turn of events, but she wanted to surprise him—and tell him in person.

Still, not finding him in would have been a bigger surprise, one she had definitely *not* counted on.

Luckily, she didn't have to. The receptionist, Ruby, smiled at her broadly when she asked if Steve was in.

"Yes, he is."

The woman was about to pick up her phone to notify Steve that he had someone waiting for him in the hall, but Erin stopped her.

"I want to surprise him," she said with such enthusiasm that Ruby allowed her to break the rules and waved her on in.

"You're not going to believe this," Erin declared once she let herself into the office and shut the door, leaning against it as she made her announcement. Her heart was hammering wildly in her chest. She'd rushed over here the moment she'd gotten the news.

"Believe what?" Steve asked innocently as he allowed himself a minute just to appreciate the very sight of her. Her cheeks were glowing and her hair was just the tiniest bit windblown. His mind started weaving fantasies and he found that he had to really struggle to keep his thoughts in check.

"Wade's lawyer just came by our office to tell me that Wade has decided to drop the suit," she told him, still stunned that the threat was really over.

"Oh?"

"Yes. According to the lawyer, Wade said some crazy man made him see the error of his ways and he wanted me to know that he wasn't going to be bothering me anymore. That he'd made a mistake about Tex and the other dinosaurs, that they weren't anything like the characters he'd been thinking of putting out."

Steve saw a mixture of elation and confusion in her eyes. "So I guess that's it," he concluded. "You won't be needing my services anymore."

That *hadn't* been the first thing she'd thought of. Actually, she hadn't thought of that consequence at all. Now that he'd mentioned it, though, she had to.

"I guess not." Erin paused, wondering if he was subtly telling her that he wasn't going to be seeing her any longer. But right now she had another question to clear up. "Would you know anything about this?"

"About what?" he asked as innocently as he could.

The look on his face almost clinched it for her. This was his doing—she'd bet on it.

"About the crazy person who made Wade see the error of his ways?"

It was growing more and more difficult for him not to laugh. "Why would I?"

"Well, for one thing," she told him, "I don't see

Wade as the type to suddenly have an epiphany in the middle of the street."

Steve shrugged. "Maybe it wasn't in the middle of the street. Maybe he had the epiphany in the bar. Or in the foyer of his apartment building."

The last detail had her eyeing Steve even more suspiciously. "How would you know he had a foyer?"

This time the shrug didn't look quite so innocent to Erin. "Just a guess. Does he?"

She wasn't buying this innocent act anymore. "It *was* you, wasn't it?"

"Was me what?" Steve bit back a grin.

She saw right through him. "You made him drop the suit."

Steve grew serious now. What Baker had tried to do was nothing more than a crime. "It wasn't a suit— it was blackmail disguised as a suit."

She smiled warmly at him. He'd made a difference in her life and no matter what lay ahead, she was always going to be grateful to him for that. "Did I tell you that I'm going ahead with that lawyer dinosaur? I'm thinking of calling him Steve."

"What happened to Clarence Darrow-Dinosaur?" he asked.

"I like Steve better," she answered.

He nodded. "Kind of partial to that myself," he commented. "Listen, since I'm not your lawyer anymore, what do you say to going out and celebrating your victory?"

"I'd love it," she said enthusiastically. Her next question completely caught him off guard—and fur-

ther convinced him that he was *so* right about this
woman. "You're bringing Jason with you, right?"

"Just clear up something for me first," he requested. "Is my seven-year-old son going to give me
some competition?"

Steve Kendall was a man who *had* no competition.
"Not a chance." She laughed.

"Then yes, I'll bring him along with me. With us,"
he corrected because the pronoun sounded so good
out loud. "Where would you like to go to celebrate?"
he asked, then named several high-class restaurants
that were in the area.

"Well," she said, "to be honest, I was actually
thinking more along the lines of going to the Orange Country Fair."

"You like deep-fried food?" he questioned in disbelief. In his experience, that was practically all there
was to eat at the fair.

"I wasn't thinking of food," she told him. "I was
thinking about the various rides. I think Jason would
have a lot of fun going on some of them."

He smiled into her eyes. "I think Jason would have
fun being anywhere as long as you were there, too."

Erin looked at him, touched as well as surprised.
"What a sweet thing to say."

"I have a lot of good qualities I'd like to show
you," he told her.

They hadn't reached the end of their relationship,
she thought in relief. She intended to remain in this
for the long haul, however long—or short—that actually was. "Sounds good to me."

"And," Steve went on, never taking his eyes off

her, "I'd like to spend the rest of my life showing you what they are."

Stunned, she stared at him. "Just what are you saying?" Erin asked.

For once in her life she was afraid to let her imagination take off without any restraints on it. Afraid that because she wanted something so very much, failing to get it would be too devastating. So she waited for an answer, refusing to provide it herself, no matter how tempting.

He paused for a moment, picking up the phone receiver and calling the receptionist out front.

"Ruby, hold my calls until further notice." He didn't wait for the receptionist to acknowledge the instruction, hanging up instead.

He looked at the woman sitting before him. At times, he was still convinced he had dreamed her up. She fit *that* perfectly into his world.

When Steve finally spoke, he chose his words carefully.

"I was one of those guys who was certain that love came just once in a lifetime—if it came at all. I'd had my once. But because I had a son who needed a mother, I made myself start looking for someone who would be able to fill that position.

"What I found instead were a lot of women—beautiful, intelligent women—who had no desire to share their lives on a long-term basis with a man who had a child. They were far too interested in their careers and themselves to venture beyond that. After a few months of trying to get back into the swing of things, I decided I didn't *want* to swing. That I'd had my one true love and I was just out of luck.

"And then you happened by when I least expected it. You with your boundless imagination and your empathy and that heart of yours that seemed as big as the great outdoors. You made me rethink my planned exodus into a hermitage."

"Hermitage?" she echoed, doing her best not to laugh out loud—and failing.

He pretended to be affronted by her laughter. "What's so funny?"

Her eyes danced with humor as she said, "You're probably just about the last person I would peg to be a hermit."

He didn't know about that. There were times, when he wasn't reviewing legal maneuvers, when he felt completely alone and adrift. Especially when he couldn't even connect with his own son. But Erin had changed all that for him.

"Well, my heart certainly felt as if it had gone into isolation—before I met you."

"Your heart," she echoed. He sounded so serious just now it made her wonder if he was trying to tell her something that she was missing.

"Yes, my heart." He blew out a frustrated breath. He could argue legal terms for hours, but this, apparently, he wasn't very good at. "Woman, I'm trying to tell you that I love you."

Stunned, she felt her jaw slacken and drop open for a second. Closing it again, Erin stared at him, not sure if she should laugh or cry.

Finally she said, "You're a lawyer, all right. Using

a hundred words when all you needed to use were three."

"Three," he repeated, closely watching her, waiting for illumination.

She nodded. "Three. The only three words any woman wants to hear."

He rose and came around his desk to her side. "'Here's my money'?" Steve pretended to guess, biting his tongue.

She rose to her feet, as well, not content to remain seated with him looming over her like this. Getting up, she was aware that there was very little space between them.

"Not even close, you idiot. The three words are *I love you, too.* Maybe four words."

"And do you?" he asked, his words all but caressing her skin as he waited for her answer.

The smile began in her eyes and worked its way down to her lips. "What do you think?"

This felt good, he told himself. It felt right. Any hesitation that might have been died before it ever had a chance to flourish. "I think if you turn this into a quiz, I'm going to explode."

"Can't have that," she said, then continued, "Yes, I love you. I think I fell in love with you in that classroom that first day when I saw that you looked so nervous talking to a classroom full of kids. It showed me that it was important to you to do a good job. Since your audience was comprised of seven- and eight-year-olds, I thought that was particularly endearing."

He shrugged off the compliment even though it

warmed him to the nth degree. "I just didn't want to embarrass Jason."

"Which was all part of the 'endearing' concept I was talking about," she told him. "It meant you regard him—and them—as people. Little people, but people just the same. That's a very good quality to have."

"Speaking of Jason, which of us should tell him about this?"

He noticed her eyes were dancing again. In a moment, he found out why.

"By 'us' do you mean you, me or Tex?"

He had to be honest with her. "I really didn't figure the dinosaur into this." He grinned and shook his head. The woman was definitely different, he mused. He was looking forward to a lifetime with her. "I guess that I should start the discussion, huh?"

"At least the first sentence or two," she encouraged. "But to answer your question, my suggestion would be that both of us should tell him that he's getting a stepmom. Tex can just hang out in the background, you know, speak only when he's spoken to."

He laughed and shook his head in wonder at the way her mind worked.

"This is definitely going to take some getting used to," he told her. "It never occurred to me that I might be welcoming a dinosaur as part of the family."

"Which is why it pays to be open to new things," she said, weaving her arms around his neck.

He smiled down at her. "Well, I'm all for that," he said with feeling.

"Good." There was an impish smile on her face.

"Because more than likely, there'll be a lot of 'that' in our life together."

"I can hardly wait," he told her, uttering exactly one word in between each kiss that he grazed across her lips.

"Me, neither," she murmured before she just lost herself in the sweet taste of his lips.

* * * * *

COMING NEXT MONTH FROM

H HARLEQUIN®

SPECIAL EDITION

Available June 24, 2014

#2347 FROM MAVERICK TO DADDY
Montana Mavericks: 20 Years in the Saddle! • by Teresa Southwick
Rust Creek Falls newcomer Mallory Franklin is focused on providing a stable home for her adopted niece—*not* finding the man of her dreams. But Mallory just can't help running into ravishing rancher Caleb Dalton everywhere she goes! Still, she's got to stand firm. After all, carefree Caleb isn't exactly daddy material...or is he?

#2348 A WIFE FOR ONE YEAR
Those Engaging Garretts! • by Brenda Harlen
When Daniel Garrett and Kenna Scott swap "I do"s in Las Vegas, the old friends know the deal. This marriage is just to help Daniel access his trust fund, and it will be dissolved before they even know it. But, as the hunk and the blonde beauty find out, their marriage of convenience might just turn into a lifelong love—and a forever family.

#2349 ONE TALL, DUSTY COWBOY
Men of the West • by Stella Bagwell
Nurse Lilly Lockett is on a mission—to heal the patriarch of the Calhoun ranching clan. Then she meets the irresistibly rakish Rafe Calhoun, the ranch's foreman. Love has burned Lilly in the past, but the remedy for her heartbreak might just lie in the freewheeling bachelor she's tried so hard to resist!

#2350 SMALL-TOWN CINDERELLA
The Pirelli Brothers • by Stacy Connelly
Debbie Mattson always put family first—until now. The beautiful baker has finally reached a point in her life where she can enjoy herself. But there's a roadblock in the way—a big, *hunky* one in the form of her lifelong friend Drew Pirelli. Drew's got it bad for Debbie, but can he help her build her happily-ever-after?

#2351 A KISS ON CRIMSON RANCH
by Michelle Major
Sara Wellens has *had* it with Hollywood! The former child star is dead broke, until she finds out she inherited part of her late grandmother's Colorado ranch. There, Sara butts heads with former bull rider Josh Travers, who wants to make the ranch a home for himself and his daughter. Has the single cowboy met his match in a former wild child?

#2352 THE BILLIONAIRE'S NANNY
by Melissa McClone
Billionaire AJ Cole needs to ward off his family's prying, so he produces an insta-girlfriend—his assistant, Emma Markwell. The brunette charmer agrees to play along, but fantasy turns to reality as the two share passionate kisses. When AJ claims he just wants a fling, Emma resists. Can she show the tycoon that she's all he needs—now and forever?

YOU CAN FIND MORE INFORMATION ON UPCOMING HARLEQUIN® TITLES, FREE EXCERPTS AND MORE AT WWW.HARLEQUIN.COM.

HSECNM0714

Looking to create his own legacy, Daniel Garrett wanted out of the family business. But the only way to gain access to his trust fund was to get married. So he convinced his best friend, Kenna Scott, to play the role of blushing bride. What could go wrong when they sealed their "vows" with a kiss that set off sparks?

***

"You set out the terms," she reminded him. "A one-year marriage on paper only."

"What if I want to renegotiate?" he asked.

Kenna shook her head. "Not going to happen."

"You know I can't resist a challenge."

Her gaze dropped to the towel slung around his waist and her breath hitched.

She moistened her lips with the tip of her tongue, drawing his attention to the tempting curve of her mouth. And he was tempted.

One simple kiss had blown the boundaries of his relationship with Kenna to smithereens and he didn't know how to reestablish them. Or even if he wanted to.

"Aren't you the least bit curious about how it might be between us?"

"No," she said, though her inability to meet his gaze made him suspect it was a lie. "I'd prefer to maintain my unique status as one of only a handful of women in Charisma who haven't slept with you."

"I haven't slept with half as many women as you think," he told her. "And I know what you're doing."

"What?"

"Deflecting. Trying to annoy me so that I stop wondering what you're wearing under that dress."

She shook her head, but the hint of a smile tugged at the corners of her mouth. "There's French toast and bacon in the oven, if you want it."

"I want to know if you really wear that stuff."

"No, I just buy it to take up storage space and torture your imagination."

"You're a cruel woman, Mrs. Garrett."

She tossed a saucy smile over her shoulder. "Have a good day, Mr. Garrett."

When Kenna left, he poured himself a mug of coffee and sat down with the hot breakfast she'd left for him.

He had a feeling the coming year was going to be the longest twelve months of his life.

***

Don't miss
A WIFE FOR ONE YEAR *by award-winning author*
Brenda Harlen, the next book in her new
Harlequin® Special Edition miniseries
THOSE ENGAGING GARRETTS!
On sale August 2014,
wherever Harlequin books are sold.

HARLEQUIN®

SPECIAL EDITION

Life, Love and Family

Coming in August 2014

ONE TALL, DUSTY COWBOY
by *USA TODAY* bestselling author
Stella Bagwell

Nurse Lilly Lockett is on a mission—to heal the patriarch of the Calhoun ranching clan. There, she meets the irresistibly rakish Rafe Calhoun, the ranch's foreman. Love has burned Lilly in the past, but the remedy for her heartbreak might just lie in the freewheeling bachelor she's tried so hard to resist!

**Don't miss the latest edition of the
Men of the West miniseries!**

*Look for THE BABY TRUTH,
already available from the
MEN OF THE WEST miniseries by Stella Bagwell!*

Available wherever books and ebooks are sold!

www.Harlequin.com

HSE65831